INDIAN MASONRY

First Edition 1907
Robert C. Wright

New Edition 2022
Edited by Tarl Warwick

INDIAN MASONRY

COPYRIGHT AND DISCLAIMER

FOREWORD

This text is an intriguing look at the quasi-Masonic practices and tales of various tribes of "Native" Americans across the United States- it is a partially romanticist work, definitively involving a sort of "noble savage" notion of the pre-industrial lives of the "red man" in contrast to the seemingly empty urban life of the "pale faces." It contains some interesting illustrations, and in part was informed by ethnographic materials from the US government, which by the dawn of the 20th century was beginning to order increasing studies regarding the decreasing population of aboriginal people.

The tales themselves (and some poetry) are interesting as well- a lot of the lore deals with medicine men and the practices of initiation into orders which are here compared to the Freemasons, usually with an eye to establishing similarity between the two. At times the connections are oddly apt, at other times, a bit of logical stretching is in order to reconcile the observed.

The fundamental question of the presence of Masonry among these people is effectively answered "yes" in the practical sense, and "no" in the organized, monotheistic sense.

This edition of "Indian Masonry" has been carefully edited for format and content. Care has been taken to retain all original intent and meaning.

INDIAN MASONRY

PREFACE

To the Brethren of the Craft:

This work is fraternally dedicated to you. In your kindly charge it is placed, hoping that when it has been measured by the plumb, square and level, it will be found good work, true work, square work, and just such work as you need and may pass to be used in the building up of the real Masonic structure.

The field of study among the aboriginal races of the new world is intensely interesting, and so much so that the author would fain do more and more in that field, could he have the time at his disposal, for he firmly believes that the Craft of this country owes it to itself to have this work done. He also believes that facts may yet be found out there, which will make our Masonry look like a Broadway store building beside an old Egyptian temple. Astonishing and curious things of the past not only fascinate and interest, but lure one on to seek to dispel the shadows cast about them and to view them in the light by which those people worked.

When facts are served up ready for mental absorbing, the average reader does not grasp the great labor it takes to gather, analyze and arrange them for his intellectual repast, even in so humble an effort as the present one. The writer offers no apology, and, according to his ability and honest efforts, he has never hesitated to do his full share of work for the best interests of the Craft wheresoever dispersed, and so he hopes always to do. Yet one easily sits down to a meal purchased for one-half dollar, coin of the realm, absorbs it with almost no effort on his part, and takes no thought of the labor it took and the number of people concerned to get up that meal for him, so he may not starve his physical being. The price obtains for him a good meal, but it lasts only a few hours, when he is forced to buy another, willy nilly. Now he is not, or thinks he is not, obliged to encourage those who would labor just as faithfully to set before him suitable and growth-making mental food, as he is to yield his patronage to those who cater to his bodily wants. These things are said, because, when the publishers took up the matter of putting this modest little work before the brethren, they mournfully and frankly said that unfortunately the Masonic fraternity did not buy freely, and what they did buy, they seem to want at very low prices for even the most meritorious Masonic works prepared for them at great labor.

The author is enthusiastic in work of this kind and would like to go on with it in other directions, but he is not a wealthy man, has many arduous duties in his profession to take his time, even while doing the present work, and must labor to keep his establishment in order daily, and support those dependent upon him. Neglect these matters he cannot, unless his income outside of the work there bestowed permits him to do so. Neither can the publishers afford to put out even a most excellent work if the Craft refuse to read anything at all. These are plain, unvarnished statements and any brother who stops for a moment to read them and thinks it over, understands it perfectly. Neither the author nor the publishers are looking for an imperial palace on the grand avenues of the world metropolis, a magnificently equipped steam yacht, or a luxuriantly furnished train for traveling. The sensible man, however, well knows that to do a work of this kind conscientiously, thoroughly, and with good results, which is the only way the author chooses to do it, he must be freed from some part of his daily burdens, and must have opportunity to leave his residence and go to places where information is to be had to the best advantage, as we prefer to investigate on the ground. Bricks cannot be made unless one gathers clay, and that he must go after in the clay grounds.

The publishers are also inspired by the same high motives, to put forth better and better work each year. Therefore, having fairly stated the position of author and publisher, it lies with the Craft whether they shall liken themselves to the Holy Saints John, and become separately and unitedly patrons of those who earnestly seek to do Masonry good and upbuild it, or shall deny their encouragement and allow it to grovel in the slough of mercenary despond where it has been for a long time past, despite the efforts of the faithful ones.

Craftsmen, while making our search for that which is lost, into your hands we commend ourselves and our work for encouragement to future efforts and the wished for benefits to thousands of Masons throughout our glorious country and elsewhere.

In conclusion, we acknowledge an indebtedness for valuable information to Prof. Powell's interesting articles written for the U. S. Government, and to those of his associates, Dr. Hoffmann, Erminie A. Smith, Garrick Mallery, James Mooney, Yarrow, Mrs. Matilda C. Stevenson, and others. Besides these we have also derived much benefit during our study from Inman, Brinton, Bancroft, Heckethom, Dellenbaugh, Schoolcraft, Bourke, Lyman, and others. Mr. Geo. H. Himes, the genial and ever industrious Secretary of the Oregon State Historical Society has helped considerably toward getting track of persons and information desired. Many other kind friends have also furnished items which proved interesting. If all sources from which we have drawn are not mentioned, due gratitude is expressed for what has been received and used.

The Author.
Portland, Oregon, September, 1907.

INDIAN MASONRY

I

INTRODUCTION

Some time ago a brother said one day that he had seen Indians give Masonic signs, and this being doubted in spite of the brother's earnestness, an investigation was begun. Much care and mental work have made progress slow and difficult, yet the odd hours which could be taken aside from a busy profession, to gather material, were most pleasantly and profitably spent. From the mass of material, a part must be chosen which will not overlap the reasonable limits of this book, but certain it is, much of great interest must be left out. What is of profit to one must be surely of profit to another, and having taken to heart the lessons these things teach, they may prove of equal benefit to others. The whole object of this work is not merely to examine the ceremonies and traditions of the Indians, for the sake of curiosity, but to fix our thought upon what they have done, what we have done, and what it all means. In other words, the writer expects to force the mind which has the least inclination to shirk its duty- to think; to arouse itself and press forward with doubled vigor. It is worth your effort, brother, quite as much as to work for a roof over you or clothes upon your body. It is the sincere purpose of this book to spread true Masonic light and set the brethren thinking, even though they reach different conclusions from the same facts.

To answer the question, Is there Masonry among the Indians, let us first try to make sure what we mean by Masonry; then find out whether the Redman had or has whatever that may be.

In doing so, it is well for us to take a square look in the mirror, and behold the face of our own Masonry and its shortcomings. Let us fear not plain speech and searching gaze, for 'tis thus only shall we see that Masonry is indeed a progressive science.

There is no written language of the Indian, and the task of getting his true thoughts and philosophy is very difficult. We must cast aside anything which betrays the hand of the white man, and as well known authorities have erred, the difficulties are only made greater.

In this work we shall deal almost wholly with the Indian who lived not in houses, the wanderer. We are used to look upon the Indian as a savage, but in its older meaning the word came from *silva*, a wood, and points to man as he was- *silvestres homines*- men of the forest or children of nature. Human nature is in nowise changed by culture. The European is but a whitewashed savage. Civilized venom is no less poisonous than that of the savage. The first may use a sweatshop, a tenement or adulterated food, the other a poisoned arrow. Let us then, when seeking a deeper insight into the ancient mysteries, not demise those things crude or seemingly of small account, but weigh them well inwardly. We can only reach the true meaning of Indian ceremonies by remembering that they see a mystery in all about us and to get as near as we can to the point from which they view the world.

Besides his language, there are two things about the Indian which are wholly unlike any other species of man. One is his isolation for time out of mind from other continents. Modem research has put into the rubbish pile all the stories about lost tribes, Japanese wanderers, etc. It seems never to occur to those who hold fast to the lost tribe and Japanese theories, that the opposite is just as probable, and that our Indians could just as easily and just as well have gone around in canoes and started the Japanese race or the Koreans. In fact the wonderful progress of the whites on this soil is better ground to believe it produced a sturdy race of Indians who are ancestors of the Japanese. The second thing is the entire absence of a herdsman's life and its softening associations. There is no reliable record of a pastoral tribe, or of animals raised for milk or transportation. I mean the old Indian, not the one of today. It was a hunting race and has all the stamp of a growth on the soil. In his own way the Indian worked out his destiny, and whatever he won was his with more than ordinary ownership. Suppose a race came here able to overpower us. The brightest and best of our kind, if unable to join that race, would be irresistibly driven, little by little, farther and farther away, leaving behind renegades, criminals and toughs, the very offscourings of our civilization. Should not the pages of history cry out against an unjust judgment of the conquering race, that such scum of the earth, in touch hand in hand with its own bad elements, was actually our people, and represented our best civilization? Even thus did the best of the Indians flee before us, leaving behind their vilest and meanest. Judge not in this wise lest in time ye be also judged in the same way. When we consider him as a hunter in constant pursuit of game, then in a very small way we may more easily understand his bloody ceremonies, his restlessness and revengeful spirit of which we read, but let us not forget the great charity and some other good qualities he displayed, for it is said an Indian never let a peaceful stranger go hungry from his tepee as long as he had com or venison to give. The white man's selfishness did much to make him bad. He was in most things a child man.

Look at the picture of the Indian whose face has been taken as a frontispiece for this work. It is Pop-Kio-Wina, or Short-Arm, a Yakima Indian of full blood. This man, who died some five or six years ago, was not a chief, but stamped upon those strong features is the imprint of generations before him, gifted undoubtedly with strong personality. Idiots and weaklings do not send down pure and vigorous blood any more than water flows up hill. This man had not been taught all that was taught his fore-fathers, because the white man's way was accepted by him. Yet, he is a man of his race, showing a strong mind in himself and his fathers, so that if there is one example of such, there were in the olden days many more like him, and thus there were bright Indian intellects in the councils of his nation, learned in the things we are now studying.

II

BROTHERHOOD

Man loves man's company, and solitude is not natural, so he seeks a neighbor, a town, a teeming city, and it is this inborn drawing of man to man that fills him with the desire for secret societies whose object is to bring him nearer to the great beyond, whose object is and should be for all members to faithfully till the soil of the great brotherhood, first among themselves, that they may thereafter be fit laborers in the greater field of the whole world. The ancient Egyptian priests had their secret societies which sought the way to the unknown country, and, in modem times, Masonry has striven to fulfill this ancient yearning of man for lodges or societies having their different cults.

Speculative Masonry teaches that there is a Grand Architect of the Universe, and points out that there must be an inner life, which goes on after what we call death or the separation of the soul from the body; that Masonry seeks to bring together all its members in the great brotherhood of man; that it strives after eternal truths. These things are taught by symbols and story for time out of mind, and with them the Grand Orient of France lays stress upon the right of free thought.

And of these, the great brotherhood of man- what is it? Our Masonry says: "By the exercise of brotherly love we are taught to regard the whole human species as one family, the high and the low, the rich and the poor, who, as created by one Almighty Parent, and inhabitants of the same planet, are to aid, support and protect each other. On this principle, Masonry unites men of every country, sect and opinion and causes true friendship to exist among those who might otherwise have remained at a perpetual distance."

A very nice abstract statement, but go further- into the great world. An infant, a few weeks old, is left upon a doorstep by the mother, who for some reason, God only knows, puts it there. She sounds an alarm and is swiftly away, eagerly watching to see if it shall be taken in from the cold blasts of winter. The door opens, the light streams forth and a man with stern, forbidding face, looks upon the bundle curiously, takes it up, hears the little cry! Will he or his wife put that little unknown stranger helpless and alone, out into the street and the cold, dark night again? Never. Why? Because the brotherhood of man within him rises to the surface, commanding him to keep a human being safely until it can be cared for by others if he will no longer do so.

A great crowd of pleasure seekers are hurrying homeward, jostling, laughing, tired, cross or good-natured, as it may be. Suddenly, above all the tumult is heard the voice of a little child, crying bitterly in that great crowd, swirling and rushing in the city's street. He is lost, lost- and as his cry goes up in pitiful tones of agonized fear and sadness, many spring to the child's side to find out his grief and help him. In all those thousands, there is not one in his right mind, no matter how low or vicious he might be, who would deny that child the aid it needs until better cared for. Many would spring to the spot with open arms. Why? 'Tis the power of that great something we call brotherly love which moves foot to foot and with hand to back.

George Catlin, the painter and writer, once wrote: "Unaided and unadvised, I resolved to use my art and so much of the labors of my future life as might be required, in rescuing from oblivion the looks and customs of the vanishing races of native men in America, to which end I plainly saw they were hastening before the approach and certain progress of civilization." More than six hundred pictures and valuable writings are now safely placed in the Smithsonian Institute as his monument. It was he who wanted "A Nation's Park," containing man and beast in all the wildness and freshness of their nature's beauty. He wanted the Redman to have one spot he might call his own. Thus in another way did George Catlin feel the thrill of true brotherhood in common with an unfortunate race.

A Roosevelt and other right minded men of our country are patiently and courageously fighting for ways and means to stop the secret, as well as the open, taking away and hoarding up of this earth and the fullness thereof, by those to whom it belongeth not.

Men and women with bright, intelligent minds, in Russia, bare their breasts and risk their lives before bayonets and bullets, or risk their liberty for Siberian prisons, in order that an autocracy, sitting on its throne for three hundred years, shall be forced to listen to a demand for a rightful government. Why? Because all these heard the mighty cry of the common people, their brothers, and answered it.

Lewis and Clarke never could have reached the Oregon country with their small company, if all the Indians on the way had been savage and hostile. Why? Because they were spurred to their task by a sincere intent to treat the Indians as men and brothers, not to rob and deceive them. So they had no trouble in finding the friendly Indians, whose help gave us the splendid Northwest Territory, which shall be greater even than any kingdom Solomon ever dreamed of, in all his glory as told in the traditions of history.

Man is but a grown-up child, and while he still hears the piercing cry of a child, or the forced shriek of an injured grown-up, his brotherhood sense has passed from that beautiful keenness of his own childhood into a blunted, dull and selfish nature, and because of this he is no longer quick to hear the far sadder, still and inmost cry from the sorely tried and distressed souls of the grown-up children about him, seeking help just as wistfully and needing it quite as much as the little child. To be able to give help in such cases, is to have within us the true brotherhood of man. We are told the number five alludes to the five senses, and of these hearing, seeing and feeling are Masonically considered most important. For many years philosophers have said there is a sixth sense, and so there is- greater than all the others. When rightly tuned, it hears heart cries which fall unheeded on ears of clay that hear not; it sees the storms of life and signs of distress in a troubled heart, where dull eye of flesh is blind; it feels the thrill of desire to battle for justice to the oppressed; and it feels a boundless sympathy stretching forth to encourage the struggling fighter in life's stream, and sheds rays of light on the sorrowing; while mortal body is unmoved by any touch which will recognize a brother in the dark as well as in the light. O, greater than them all, and all in one!

Can we, with the grips we now have, raise this deadened master sense to a bright and living perpendicular, or must we look for some other grip we know not and for light we have not received? O, Masonry, let thy actions, not thy words, tell the world that thou hast light abundantly!

Brotherhood is a mysterious inner being which moves freely as water; is man's every day need and without which he cannot live or be happy. Like water, always water, whether it be found in fairest flower or fruit, or in terrible poison, in foul or in rotten mass; it spreads in great or little streams throughout all mankind as one. Now sluggishly, ebbing away to lowest depths, where are the swamps of stupidity or slimy baseness within the minds of those unlearned or of gross and beastly nature. Yet ceaselessly at work, changing those to whom it comes, purifying and lifting them up, until at last it rises in kingly splendor, like soft and beautiful clouds in the blue sky, from whence again it gently cometh in all its purity to where mean, rank or coarse growths are founds; again to where the waving grains of industry and kindly fruits of charity and truth in valley and plain are seen. Yet again to where rare and beautiful flowers of learned and wise minds may be found, high on the mountain side of a good life, to be seen and known in all their worth- only by the few. Whether we find brotherhood in minds like lofty mountains, joyous, rippling streams, or in ocean's vast depths of wisdom- 'tis ever, the same mighty life stream of brotherhood of man, which seeks its way on the level of time and flows thus unto itself again and again, it matters not where or how widely apart man from man may be on this earth, for one touch of it proves all the world is kin.

Science and religion are agreed upon the theory of monogenism or the specific unity of man, and reason bids us put away a prejudice that natural religions are as the old philosophers taught, or as the dark ages imagined; subtle nets of the devil spread to catch human souls. With the Redman, it was his unhelped reaching out to do what others have done- to find out God; a yearning after Kitshi Manido whom we call the Grand Architect, and thus his efforts are not idle fancies any more than ours, but worthy of study. 'Tis the brotherhood in man which makes us reach forth in a firm belief that there is something, an innermost personality, which outlives our present and carries it into another world. This thought is spread among all mankind and is inborn in the human mind.

It is well proven that the mind of man is but a common substance, and thoughts and ideas of the same kind flow freely throughout the vast sea of mind, divided only seemingly by bodies which are like vessels holding but portions of that which is in fact joined as of the whole. It is not uncommon for two persons to apply for a patent on the same invention. They are far apart and do not know each other or each other's work until the patent office tells them, and still others may have had the same idea who never made it known there. It is the same with writers. Shakespeare stole his plots and ideas from his forerunners. Masonry has done the same. In Pliny's Nat. Hist, Bk. ii, c. 63, probably written in 77

A.D., is this passage: "Next comes the earth, on which alone of all parts of nature we have bestowed the name that implies maternal veneration. It is appropriated to man as the heavens are to God. She receives us at our birth, nourishes us when born and afterwards supports us in her bosom; when we are rejected by the rest of nature, she then covers us with especial tenderness." Does this writing of a so-called pagan sound familiar to the Masonic ear? The Indian likewise has these same ideas. In his ceremonies he made a smoke offering, by dipping his pipe, to Nokomis, the earth, the grandmother of mankind, for the benefits which are derived from her body, where they were placed by Kitshi Manido.

If man did not borrow that which is best and improve it there would be no progress. Yet we call it plagiarism or stealing of ideas. When an electric current flows through one wire, it often changes or influences another current flowing through a nearby wire. Thus an idea may start in one mind and, through that wonderful unity of man, cast its influence over and appear in other minds at the same time or ages hence. Place iron filings on a paper and hold a magnet below. A mysterious power causes the filings to arrange themselves in circle after circle, all attracted toward a common center, making what we call the magnetic field. Let the Mason who talks about the point within the circle call to mind then, that every movement, whether for good or evil, which affects mankind starts from a common center and spreads outwardly. Let a great wrong threaten the land or a calamity befall a neighborhood. Some leader sees it early and from him starts a great magnetic wave of patriotism or charity, which may sweep through minds all over the country- aye and the world! These things being so, there must be one great cause eternal from whom all things flow.

INDIAN MASONRY

III

SIGNS

I have had Masons solemnly tell me that they had seen Masonic signs given by Indians and that they were Masons. This can be explained in two ways: first, the Indian had actually become a Mason or had learned the signs secretly from white men as negroes of the south have done; second, those brethren had taken as Masonic, signs made by the Indian for which he intended an entirely different meaning. There is great danger that the civilized understanding is mistaken or forced, and errors are more likely to happen from the hearsay of traders, interpreters and agents, who have made an Indian jargon, and insist that signs of their own making, adopted by the Indians, are universal. This failure to interpret correctly is well set forth in the old Scotch story of King James I, who desired to play a trick upon the Spanish ambassador, whose hobby was sign language, so told him of a great professor of that science at Aberdeen. The King sent ahead for the professors to make the best of him. A droll wag of a butcher, having one blind eye, was dressed in gown and provided with glasses; then told to use only signs. The ambassador went into the room to see this man and came out quite pleased that his theory was proven. He said: "I raised one finger, meaning there is one God. He answered by raising two, which was to say this being rules over two worlds, material and spiritual, and I raised three, meaning there are three persons in the trinity, upon which he closed his fingers to say these three are one." Then the professors sent for the butcher who was very angry and said: "When the crazy mon came in he raised one finger as much as to say I had but one eye, and I raised twa fingers to mean I could see out of one eye as weel as he out of both of them. Then he raised three fingers as much as to say there were but three eyes between us. Then I doubled up my feest and if he had not gang out in a hurry I would have knocked him doon."

INDIAN MASONRY

In the matter of signs it is possible to pantomime so that anyone will understand a skillful representation of a tailor, blacksmith; drawing water and drinking, etc. It is necessary to distinguish between a sign which is merely to help us carry on conversation or recognize a brother, and a sign which stands not alone for some object or action, but for some occult and mystic meaning, and needs explanation from history, religion or custom. The ark, dove, olive branch or rainbow, mean nothing to us unless we know Mosaic history. An emblem is yet farther away. We have our familiar square and compasses in the position usually seen, and it is known as a Masonic emblem when on our coats or watch charms. A flag stands to represent our sovereignty and the Indian has a like tribal or totemic sign; but all these are not symbols in the manner thus used. An attempt to make out of Indian signs much that is symbolic or stands for hidden meaning will fail. The Northern Pacific Railway uses for its business a sign like a trademark, well known to us all by sight. It consists of two different-colored, comma-like characters interlapped so that they lie wholly within a circle, and is really a very ancient symbol of Chinese phallic religion. Suppose in five hundred years from now the railway is out of existence and forgotten; but some scientist of that day discovers specimens of its literature or the side of a car bearing this character. Would it not be absurd for wise men to say that the railway was the custodian and teacher of some mysterious cult, instead of the character being merely used as an emblem, company, or business sign? Of course the religion of secret rebates to the beef trust cannot fairly be included as a cult under shelter of this ancient symbol.

The best authorities appear to agree, that as early as man became possessed of all his faculties, he did not choose between voice and gesture, both being instinctive always. Neither did he use one of these faculties and allow the other to be dormant. At first he imitated the sounds of nature with his voice and with gestures he showed actions, motions, positions, forms, dimensions, directions, distances, etc. It would therefore seem that oral speech, however, lagged behind, after gesturing had become a finished accomplishment. It must be admitted that the connection between voice and gesture was so close at an early period, that gestures in the wide sense of presenting ideas under physical forms had a direct effect in forming many words. Gestures exhibit the earliest condition of the human mind, and, traced from the remotest time among all peoples having records, are generally found among savages, survive in scenic pantomime, and still accompany ordinary speech of civilized man by motions of the head, face, hands and body, often involuntary, often purposely, in illustration or for emphasis.

Signs as well as words, animals and plants have their growth, development and change, their births, and deaths; a struggle for existence with a survival of the fittest. It is probable, however, that their radicals can be learned with more accuracy than those of words. Professor Whitney of Yale College says: "A word is a combination of sounds, which by a series of historical reasons has come to be accepted and understood in a certain community as the sign of a certain idea. As long as they so accept, it has existence." We know well that our dictionaries contain many an obsolete word, which if used in ordinary conversation would be wholly meaningless except to scholars who had spent their lives in the study of language.

There is ample evidence in the pages of history, beside that from other sources, that the regular use of signs for conversation is of great antiquity. The value of gestures and particularly with the fingers is shown by their extended use among modem Italians, to whom they have directly descended. The Indians have been able to understand a great deal of the sign language of deaf mutes. However, what is a mere adjunct or accomplishment to the Indian is a necessity to the deaf-mute and is his natural mode of expressing himself. It is therefore not surprising that each should adopt signs for many things which the mind of either savage or civilized man would naturally select. That sign language was as universal in North America as elsewhere cannot be doubted. Quintillian says, (1. xi, c. 3): "In tanta per omnes gentes nationesque linguae diversitate hic mihi omnium hominum communis sermo videatur." Michaelius, writing in 1628, says of the Algonquins on or near Hudson river: "For purposes of trading, as much was done by signs with the thumb and fingers as by speaking," and other authorities say the same.

The Indian has his medicine men and chiefs, who are leaders and form a smaller sect, for the old, old search for light and that which was lost. In every tribe there is a great body of story lore which they claim to be the sayings and doings of the gods and of great men. Like Masonry, they have that which is handed down, not in books. In the long winter evenings a person of the tribe skilled in such things, tells these stories from their unwritten bible to men and women, boys and girls, gathered about the camp fire. Such a scene is of the deepest interest. Before a camp fire, see the dusky faces, as an old man tells his story, the elders listening with reverence, while the younger are played upon by the actor until they shiver with fear or dance with delight. An Indian is a great actor. The Indian life trains him in natural sign language, which has spread so an Indian can talk with other tribes whose spoken language he does not understand. A skillful Indian preacher talks and acts with his face, hands, feet and muscles of his body, and, inspired by a theme which treats of the gods, he sways his savage audience at will, ever as he tells his story pointing a moral; and mythology, theology, religion, history, customs and all human duties are taught. For reasons given, it is not unusual that a sign common in many parts of the world should occur among the Indians, but this does not prove that the Indian's ancestors took any sign from the Egyptians or any other people where we may find like signs.

As already said, signs are very liable to be misunderstood; yet some of them have a startling likeness to ancient Masonic symbols. The common Indian sign for sun is to close the right hand, the index finger and thumb curved with the tips touching to form a circle and then hold the hand toward the sky. Now the circle and point within the circle are Egyptian characters for sun, and plainly show the general idea of the disk. Our own candidates are given an explanation of the point within the circle which is by no means an ancient Masonic mystery, yet carries out the brotherhood idea. The old Egyptian hieroglyph for negation was a bracket facing downward, while an Indian makes a sign for the same thing by extending his arms horizontally sideways, the hands dropping slightly, which makes the same inverted bracket. In the Romish church the priest makes the sign of the cross upon his breast, raises the host on high, bends his knee at the altar and bums incense in swinging censers. The Mason gives his signs before his altar. The Indian bums his incense in the pipe which he raises and moves in the course of the sun with solemn ceremony. Where then is the wide difference in thought or final meaning between any of these- all men? The careful student will clearly see that the Indian had no signs which were strictly symbolic, even though they may be like Egyptian or other signs which were symbolic. The Indian signs were mere emblems used when they wished to speak of the object represented and no more. Thus for a long time the famous Dakota calendar, which was a mere history of events in tribal life by dates, was explained by enthusiasts to be truly the sun religion in equations of time, and that our Indians preserved secretly the lost geometric cult of pre-cushite scientists- all of which was simply rot.

In sign language, the tribal sign or name of the Bannock Indians was given by drawing the extended index finger across the throat from left to right and out to nearly arm's length, accompanied by a whistling sound. The Bannocks are said to have cut the throats of their prisoners.

A typical Indian sign for night is to place the flat hands palm down, horizontally outward and about two feet apart, move quickly in an upward curve toward one another until the right lies across the left. This means darkness covers all night.

It can thus be readily understood that Masonic signs, which are simply gestures given to convey ideas, no doubt have taken their origin from the same signs or like signs now corrupted but which meant something different in the beginning. Were we able to trace these signs we would then at once jump to the conclusion that the people who used them were Masons the same as we ourselves. The signs which have just been mentioned as given by the Indians could easily be mistaken for Masonic signs by an enthusiastic Mason, more anxious to find what he thinks is in them than to indulge in sober analysis of the sign and its meaning.

A ceremonial sign for peace, friendship, or brotherhood was made by the extended fingers, separated, interlocked in front of the breast, the hands horizontal with the backs outward. When this sign is represented as a pictograph, we have on the Indian chart what corresponds exactly to the clasped hands on the Masonic chart, which means the same thing.

One day in the fall of 1906 I engaged Judge Thomas A. McBride, of the circuit bench of Oregon, in conversation about Indians, and was regaled with a number of interesting narratives from his experience. The Judge is a pioneer, and having been raised in their vicinity has been much among them. Unfortunately his mind as a young lad was not directed particularly to making analysis of their ceremonies and customs, and he was obliged to search his memory to find such facts as were sought for this work. In that conversation, however, he told me that among the Klickatat Indians, who inhabited the northwest, he had seen the initiation or making of an Indian doctor. He remembered particularly that the Indians seemed to hop about or dance, and gave a chant or monotonous song, which seemed to have stops or periods in it. At each of these periods the Indian head man or chief would give a sign, and at once all the Indians taking part would raise their hands above the head and drop them with a grunt. This sign might be readily mistaken for something else, as the Mason well knows.

The Judge also stated that in making a young man a warrior or member of the tribe in full standing, they danced around a deer skin, which had upon it the usual sign of the sun, or the circle with rays out-spreading. He Had also seen on the points of rocks below St. Helens, a town on the Columbia river, a similar sun sign. The locality was called by the Red- men "Kusnehi" or "place of the salmon," and the signs were made by scratching them in the moss of the rocks so they were plainly visible from the river. The Indians were loath to tell much about or explain their beliefs, but as nearly as he could get from them, this sign was to make the salmon more plentiful, but he could not say whether this was their real reason or not. In all probability, the sign Judge McBride saw was simply the pictograph for the sun, elsewhere referred to in this work, and is so old its time of origin is unknown.

Mr. Charles Frush, a Mason who spent many years among the Indians of Oregon and Washington, told me he had never seen any Masonic sign given by Indians, and if any one claimed he had seen such, it was misunderstood and was for conversational purposes. In response to an inquiry about a report that Indians who had gone east many years ago, upon re- turning to Lewiston, Idaho, had formed a Masonic lodge, Mr. T. W. Randall, Grand Secretary of A. F. & A. M. in Idaho, wrote me as follows: "I was in Lewiston as early as 1862 and heard of Indian Masons but was never able to trace this to a reliable source. I have frequently discussed this question with old pioneers of Oregon and Washington but never found a person who was a Mason, and who believed the Indians ever were Masons or had a lodge. That some tribes have certain signs by which they can recognize each other, there can be no doubt, but those signs are not Masonic signs so far as I can learn." Mr. Randall has thus correctly determined that the signs he refers to are nothing more than conversational signs. The different tribes had a sign which stood for their totem or the name of their tribe, and it is very easily understood that an Indian of the same tribe on seeing his tribal sign, would recognize the one giving it as a fellow tribesman. Indians of a different tribe, familiar with it, would also recognize the sign and in turn could give their own sign and thus each know where the other "hails from." There is nothing strange about it.

IV

MEDICINE

The doctor is always a priest and the priest always a doctor among the Indians, hence the whites make it "medicine man." Anything mysterious, sacred, or of wonderful power or efficacy in Indian life, is designated as medicine, being the nearest equivalent of the aboriginal expressions in the various tribes.

There is no doubt in the writer's mind that the Indian exerted in his methods of healing, without the use of medicines, a certain hypnotism or mind control which is quite akin to our hypnotism, and especially near to what we term "Christian Science," although the Indian was always somewhat more strenuous in his "practice."

Among the white people we find a considerable number of so-called mediums or persons said to be possessed of the power to talk with spirits which have passed to the beyond. These mediums and those who believe in them are wont to gather in societies for the purpose of holding seances. These persons usually do some few sleight-of-hand tricks or operate with confederates and it is looked upon as a wonderful performance. The usual tricks always deceive a great many of the credulous who are among us on every hand. All of this does not show that the white race is an aggregation of spiritualists, nor that the study of psychology and all kinds of strange phenomena should not be undertaken. We should neither be stubbornly credulous, nor foolishly set against examination of any and all interesting phenomena, merely because we at first find ourselves skeptical. The Indians had these mediums and spiritualists the same as we have, but this cult was more popular and had a stronger hold on the average Redman than on his white brother. The effect was the same however. There were plenty who believed in the tricks under dim lights and there were plenty who were wise and in their own minds understood and saw through it all, even if they said nothing for policy's sake.

In examination of the Indian's belief in spirits or ghosts, we must bring ourselves to look upon him as a human being and that a white man, educated to no higher degree than the Indian, would exhibit the same tendencies and the same psychic phenomena if placed in the same surroundings. One needs only to look about among our every day acquaintances to see that mind matter is alike everywhere.

It is not an easy thing to trace for the reader the wondrous workings of the human mind toward a belief in spirits or ghosts, during its progress, while the mind is vased within a body growing from childhood's simplicity to the experiences of maturer years. For the purposes of this work it is well to briefly gather up at this point and discuss the views of a most esteemed writer, as it will help us to understand the Indian better.

It is clear at the start, that the human mind does work in the periods which we call unconsciousness. This all will admit. We have the activities of the mind during sleep, when man seems to go out of himself to talk with his friends, to see strange scenes and undergo strange experiences.

Then a man seems to live a wonderfully active life, while his body is in profound repose. Sometimes these dream scenes are repeated in actual waking life, and this occasional "coming true of dreams," gives rise to a belief in them, while all other dreams are forgotten. The dreams of sleepers are therefore often credited to the person's "double." In many diseases the mind also goes out upon these strange wanderings. Sometimes on restored health the person may recall these wonderful experiences and during their occurrence the subject talks to unseen persons and seems to have replies, and to those who witness it, he seems to act in such a way that a second self, a spirit outside of the body, is suggested. We need only turn to the history of Joan of Arc to illustrate these statements. When the disease amounts to a long continued insanity, all of these effects are much exaggerated and deeply impress those who witness the phenomena. Thus, sometimes the hallucinations of fever-racked brains and mad minds are attributed to spirits.

Now these same conditions naturally produced by dreams and disease, can, to almost the same, if not wholly the same extent, be brought about by artificial means, in the practice of ecstasism.

In the fierce struggle of savage life, when little or no provision is made for the future, there are times when the savage resorts to almost anything at hand as a means of subsistence, and thus all plants, parts of plants, seeds, flowers, fruit, leaves, bark, roots, anything in times of need may be used as food. Experience then steps in and teaches the various effects upon the human system which the several vegetable substances produce, and so the effect of narcotics is early discovered. The same results of course, are produced by these drugs upon the white man's body as upon that of the Redman. The Indian and the savages of other climes, in the practice of their religion, often times resort to those native drugs, in order to produce an ecstatic state, in which divination may be performed. This practice of ecstasism is universal in the lower stages of culture. In times of great anxiety, every savage and barbarian seeks to enter into communication with his gods and learn the future. Throughout all the earlier times of mankind, ecstasism was practiced, and civilized man has thus an inherited appetite for narcotics, to which the enormous propensity to drunkenness in all nations bears witness. When Rip Van Winkle holds his goblet aloft and says, "here's to your health and to your family's and may they live long and prosper," he connects the act of drinking with a prayer, and unconsciously demonstrates the origin of the use of stimulants. It may be that when the jolly companion has become a loathsome sot, and his mind is ablaze with the fire of drink, and he sees uncouth beasts in horrid presence, that inherited memories haunt him with the beast gods worshiped by his ancestors, at the very time when the appetite for stimulants was created. The commonly known alcoholic stimulants however, were made known to the Indian by his white brother.

Ecstasism is also produced by other means, and the savage and barbarian resorts to fasting and bodily torture, as well as by other ways to bring about this wonderful state, and the visions of his ecstasy are interpreted as the evidence of spirits. Many physical phenomena serve to confuse this opinion. In savagery and barbarianism, shadows are supposed to be emanations from, or duplicates of the bodies causing the shadows, and they also suppose them to be emanations or duplications of the object reflected. They do not understand the reflection of the rays of the sun, or that the waves of the air are turned back and sound is duplicated by an echo. He thinks the echo is the voice of an unseen personage or spirit. There is nothing more thoroughly implanted in early mankind than spiritism, and we have it with us yet.

A well known writer said: "I have been in a great camp meeting where speakers stirred many on every hand by the story of the crucifixion and the joy of redemption, to be followed by conversions of those who sought to be saved. This scene, dramatic as it was, did not exceed in dramatic effect another which I witnessed in the tall evergreen forest of the Rocky Mountains, where a tribe was gathered, just as their white brethren, and the temple of light from the blazing fire was walled by the darkness of midnight. In the midst of this grandest of all temples, stood an old man, telling in simple language the story of Tawats the Great Hare, when he conquered the Sun and established the seasons and days." Religion in this stage of theism is sorcery. Incantation, dancing, fasting, bodily torture and ecstasism are practiced. No enterprise is undertaken without consulting the gods and no evil impends but they seek to propitiate the gods. All daily life to the minutest particular is religious. The Indian keeps his sacred relics, and we find those professing the religion of Christ keeping sacred relics, while the Mason likewise has some very old and sacred, dusty bric-a-brac, which he brings forth on occasion, such as his ark, rod, key, etc. These I will not at this time explain the true significance of. The white man likewise has fast-days in his religion. Superstition is just as rampant throughout the land today as it was years ago, among all peoples of the earth, only its form is more subdued and refined.

Shortly before this work goes to press, an event occurred which clearly demonstrates the smoldering savagery within the white man's breast. There is a community near Chicago known as Zion City. It was founded by one Alexander Dowie, now dead, who was a religious dreamer- a man believed to have been of unsound mind. This man so impressed his religious ideas and fancies upon thousands of susceptible people, many of whom exhibited great shrewdness in the business world, that he had a great town in existence before his death came. Naturally, understudies and branches of this turbid stream flowing from the realms of "make-believers," sprang up. Latterly a sub-sect grew up in the said community, known as Parhamites. They were repudiated by the successors of Dowie. A man named Parham, hailing from Topeka, Kansas, claimed to have had a "vision," directing him to go to Zion City and save the inhabitants. He went. He held open air meetings and soon had a cult of his own and the usual following of fanatics. A crowd of some size can always be acquired by such leaders, no matter how utterly absurd or in- sane the "visions" or purported ceremonies and ritual or beliefs may be. People can be found with surprising ease, ready to join a new society, though its tenets may be to burn down their houses because it is against the will of the Lord to have a roof over the head. They could also be just as easily found to indulge in a worship of supposed inhabitants of the moon, who dine off green cheese, and have wonderful spiritual power over men.

These Parhamites claimed to have the "gift of tongues," and that several of their number had spoken in foreign languages. In the vicinity where the writer lives, just such another sect sprang up and held forth the same pretended miraculous gifts. While attending one of the meetings of these latter persons, one evening, during the time when scoffers and unbelievers were allowed to be present, the writer observed a woman, exhibiting all the hysterical symptoms of emotional insanity, arise and in wild tones and gestures give a vivid description of hell, which she claimed to have seen. At the same time she took pains to deny that she was crazy! Her arguments to prove her sanity were simply pitiful. From personal observations it is therefore believed that the Zion sect is of the same material as the one just referred to. In the one the writer visited, children were brought under such close influence of these insane notions that the juvenile court was forced to take a young girl away from her misguided parents, in order to release her from this fanatical nonsense and put her in school where she rightfully belonged. For this the parents informed the judge that he would be punished by God!

Now the news accounts of the Parhamites indicate that they have reached the limit of fanaticism, and have descended to primitive savagery. It seems that some five of them were arrested under a charge of murder. The facts given out were that an old lady of sixty-four- a helpless rheumatic cripple for twenty years- was to be "treated" by these people, and two of those arrested were her own daughter and son! The husband, a non-believer, was lured away from the house. The five then went to the bedroom of the unfortunate victim, locked the door and knelt in prayer. During this, they must have worked themselves into the crucial frenzy required, just as much as the Indians ever did in their ghost dances.

Then, muttering incantations, they seized the distorted arms and legs of the poor old woman and ^twisted them out of their sockets. Pillows were held to her mouth to smother her feeble screams, while her emaciated body was beaten until it was bloody. They sat upon her knees until the bones cracked. Finally her life went out amid fanatical songs shrieked and yelled by these tormenters as they drowned her cries. Every bone in her legs and arms was reported to be broken and her head twisted until the neck would not support it. Her flesh was purple from bruises.

This was not the only instance, for it was noised about that other invalids had been killed in the same manner. In this case it was given out that the death was natural, but some who heard the screams caused an inquiry to be made, which resulted in the arrests.

The son testified before the coroner's jury that a man named Mitchell and his wife had a "vision" in which he was ordered to quit work and devote his time to casting out demons from the sick. The son said his mother's consent was obtained for the "treatment," and hypnotic passes were made before her face, after which the muscular force was used, and which he said was strongly resisted by the "demons."

It is possible these persons started in with notions that they could pray the rheumatism out of the old woman, and the "laying on of hands" and passes made, would drive out the demons. Then the degree of their insanity became greater, coupled with a desire to obtain their end by positive physical means if necessary, so that if by chance the victim did live through and obtain some slight use of her limbs, it could be proclaimed abroad as a "miracle" worked by them with the assistance of God. After the arrest, it seems Mitchell and others of the cult, confessed they lost control of themselves, "when possessed of devils."

Now these things happened in the year of our Lord 1907,

and in our proudly heralded country- the enlightened, civilized, progressive white man's country- not in darkest Africa, Tierra del Fuego, the islands of the sea, or yet among the remnants of our Indians. Judge McBride, to whom reference is further made in this book, told me that he was sure the Indian Medicine man who made passes and motions of seizing and pulling something out of the body of a sick man where the disease is supposed to be located, really believes he has hold of a demon, which he promptly drowns in a vessel of water nearby, and so cures the patient.

Mrs. Stevenson, who made exhaustive researches among the Zuni, tells of her efforts to protect an old dying Zuni, from the theurgists or medicine men and women. However, as death approached, several women came and took seats about the man, with the determination that the ancient customs should not be interfered with. When the old man showed the restlessness coming with near death, a doctress crossed his hands under the blankets and held them firmly, and the expression of his face told plainly his suffering, but it was only the beginning of his torture. His son prepared a mush of white corn meal and a doctress fed it to the dying man by the spoonful. With each dose she said, "Father, take this, it will feed you on the road." He was continually stuffed with the mush, which he swallowed with difficulty, until too far gone to make the effort. The doctress then held the nostrils and blew into the mouth until it was concluded life could no longer be prolonged, then another doctress began a violent kneading of the stomach to assist the spirit to free itself from the body, and two others began pressing the lips and eyelids. It was horrible to see the tortures inflicting upon the dying man who struggled for breath. Mrs. Stevenson was powerless to contend against the numbers present but finally got word to the government doctor who came, and by his stern manner and physical force, allowed the last spark of life to pass quietly away. In this incident we gain a clear insight of the origin and counterpart of the savagery of the Parhamites.

INDIAN MASONRY

Well indeed do we write it down that the white man has but a veneer over his own savage nature- thin as air, and as easily breathed aside by the mouthings of fanatics. He hears the call of those of the wild, and breaks forth in the savage moods of the very barbarians to whom his kind send Christian missionaries that they may be saved! And saved from what? Did it ever occur to our readers that if the ignorant and superstitious heathen should visit our country, they would be in crying need of a saving from contact with such "Indians" as these Parhamites and others of like ilk, lest the work done in "civilizing" our visitors all come to naught? Does it also come to mind that we have now a large, superstitious class, ready to take up these crazy cults, who need the protection of stronger minds and arms quite as much as the benighted heathen?

When the great San Francisco earthquake occurred there were preachers who proclaimed it a judgment of God upon a city buried in the wickedness of Sodom, and there were many who thought and believed this thing to be holy truth. If one stands upon the brink of a deep river and leans over too far, he knows in advance that he will, in accordance with fixed laws of nature, fall in and be drowned if he cannot swim and no help is at hand. He does not charge such an act to his God but to his own carelessness or willfulness. If a people build a great city upon made ground, near mountains which are still in their throes of formation, with faults in the earth strata, and those mountains suddenly slip and move because of these things, they will cause a violent trembling of the surrounding earth for many miles, and the made ground will swell and vibrate like jelly in a bowl. Then the city will fall and fire and destruction follow; all according to the same natural laws as at the brink of the river. In this case the people did not know just exactly how near to the brink they stood, but they did know their country was subject to earthquake disturbances. Yet, many listen not to their own common sense, or the voice of the scientist, but boldly proclaim the earthquake due to supernatural causes instead of the same laws of nature governing the man on the river's brink. Some people do not understand natural phenomena any better than the Indian, and do as he did in assigning the causes to his God.

Looking into the Holy Scriptures, which the Mason uses as a guide, we find many significant passages, which clearly indicate a belief in spiritualism, and in dreams.

It is sown a natural body; it is raised a spiritual body. There is a natural body and there is a spiritual body. I Cor. 15:2.

Now a thing was secretly brought to me, and mine ear received a little thereof.

In thoughts from the visions of the night, when deep sleep falleth upon men.

Fear came upon me, and trembling, which made all my bones to shake.

Then a spirit passed before my face; the hair of my flesh stood up.

It stood still, but I could not discern the form thereof: an image was before mine eyes, there was silence, and I heard a voice saying.

Shall mortal man be more just than God? Shall a man be more pure than his maker? Job 4: 12-17.

Referring to dreams from fasting, Isaiah says: It shall even be as when an hungry man dreameth, and behold, he eateth not; but he awaketh, and his soul is empty. Isaiah 30:8.

And he dreamed, and behold a ladder set up on the earth, and the top of it reached to heaven; and behold the angels of God ascending and descending on it. Gen. 28: 12.

This last was the familiar dream of Jacob's ladder. It is a familiar topic in Masonic monitors and shows the inclination of Masonry to turn to these same things. In passing, it may be well to say that in the great Babylonian cities there were structures which had great steps approaching them from long distances. Temples were set at the top of these long terrace-like approaches. Up and down these long flights of steps, passed men and women, and no doubt on the day of a great festival, women and girls clad in snowy white garments with wreaths upon their heads may have passed thus, while from the temple at the top, some priest may have made his religious proclamation in a loud voice, resounding through the space below. Suppose Jacob had been accustomed to witnessing such a scene as this. Would not his mind have pictured, in the deep sleep of the desert, a scene like this, and especially when his pillow was of stones? One need only to recall that it is some fantastic mingling of waking scenes which makes up the dream scenes. The ladder is no doubt due to the work of translators and so we have Jacob's Ladder reaching to heaven.

In the quotation first given from Corinthians, the very word "raised" is used. So again, we find the Mason, the Scriptures and the Indian on common ground.

Shakespeare was imbued with the same ideas and clothes them in the spoken words of his characters. Calpumia, the wife of Caesar, sees in her dreams frightful sights which portend the death of Caesar, and cause her to beg that he go not forth on that fatal day. She says:

"And graves have yawned, and yielded up their dead;
Fierce fiery warriors fight upon the clouds.
In ranks and squadrons and right form of war,
Which drizzled blood upon the Capitol;
The noise of battle hurtled in the air,

Horses did neigh and dying men did groan.
And ghosts did shriek and squeal about the streets.
O Caesar! these things are beyond all use,
And I do fear them."

Here we have the same mind phenomena pictured as we find among the Indians, the Jews, or any other white nation.

It were well, if the insincerity of the few and the superstitions of the many could be brushed away, and the clear light of day shine upon all alike. Gibbon says in his history, "The philosophers viewing with a smile of pity and indulgence, the various errors of the vulgar, diligently practiced the ceremonies of their fathers, devoutly frequented the temples of the gods, and sometimes condescending to act a part on the theater of superstition, they concealed the sentiments of the atheist under the sacerdotal robes."

Can it be possible, that in our age we have masters, wardens and officers of our lodges, who, under selfishness and a mercantile spirit, conceal a contempt for the real Masonry, and condescend to act their parts in what to them is nothing but mummery and a jumble of words, while they swell up with pride that chance and more or less wire-pulling have put them in the positions they hold?

How often, oh, how often, do we see and hear men of bright minds, who remain in a church, the narrow dogmas and traditionary rules of faith in which, bind their mental activity within unreasonable bounds. It is as though one were in a room whose four walls encased air which did not change; until the lungs, the heart, the whole vital system, longed for, cried out, panted for, and urged one toward the clearer and purer, live-giving air beyond those narrow confines. Yea, until the gasping soul, with a mighty effort, burst its bondage, and drank in with swelling breast, great drafts of live-giving ether, in that magnificent freedom of the big, wide world beyond.

V

BELIEFS AND CEREMONIES

The Indians have a word in their tongues which has no equivalent in any European tongue, yet it means the power of the unseen world, without standing for a person. It has been called spirit, demon, god, devil, mystery, etc., but commonly and absurdly in English and French, "medicine." In Algonquin it is *Manito* and *Oki*; in Iroquois, *Otkou*; in Dakota, *Wakan*; in Chinook, *Tomaniwus*. In general, all these mean that which is above the natural world- in the heavens. In Dakota, *niya* is literally breath, figuratively, life. In Yakima, *wkrisha* means there is wind, *wkrishwit*, life. We have "spiritual" and this comes from the Latin *spirare*, to blow, breathe. Pass then from the Indian and we read in our own Great Light that the spirit of God moved upon the waters; that is, a wind or breath of life. Jehovah formed man of the dust of the ground and breathed into his nostrils the breath of life. Man did not draw the idea of God from nature. Wind was identical with breath, breath with life; life with soul, and soul with God, and therein lies the truer and deeper reasoning, brought forth little by little and confirmed by the forms of language. The Indian did not have a single god as we understand, nor did he divide his gods into good and evil until the white man came.

It would seem, from conversations the writer has had with persons who have known the Indians to a large degree, that there is a well-defined opinion that missionaries threw away many splendid chances to become wholly familiar with Indian beliefs and ceremonies. The missionaries were inclined to stubbornly frown down the Indian's ideas of God and religion, and to exert every effort to suppress his old customs and performances as heathenish and ignorant. This made him conceal much of great interest from them. They also ridiculed, and, as he thought, jeered at the ways of his fathers. That hurt his pride, so he concealed everything more vigorously. Alas that the mind of man should have been so narrow, when golden opportunities in their full development were frittered away forever! And more than this, had the missionaries and traders displayed toward long cherished customs and traditions of the Indians a respect which would have gained their confidence, they would have had respect themselves for what the white man had to offer. It betokens a lack of brotherhood on the part of a race endowed with superior knowledge but of intense egotism and stubbornness.

The Indian philosopher sees that men and animals breathe and vaguely recognizes, the phenomenon of wind and that it is like breath. He declares there is a monster in the north that breathes the cold north wind; that other beasts make the winds of the south, east and west. He fails to understand that there is atmosphere surrounding the earth, and only partly gets the facts relating to the winds. His philosophy is personal, so he has four wind gods. The Norseman found he could cool his brow with a fan or kindle a fire or sweep dust with wafted air; that the wind did the same on a larger scale, and he said: Some one fans the waters of the fjord or the forests- the god Hraesvelger, clothed with eagle plumes, is spreading his wings in flight, and the winds rise from under them. The early Greek found that air may be imprisoned in vessels or move in the ventilation of caves. He saw in it more than breath or fanning, something which could be gathered up and scattered abroad, so he said: The sacks have been untied, the caves have been opened. The philosopher of civilization has the science of meteorology, which shows him an orderly succession of events even in the fickle winds. The Ute believes the sun is a living being, and he has a story of how it came. The modern philosopher places the sun as a shining globe in space and seeks out the harmonious movements of the earth and heavenly bodies. Yet the wise modern philosopher, when asked what is the soul and what is God, must stop and say, I know not! The Mason has his place of darkness in the north and follows the course of the sun from east to west and west to east again. Herein we find the great brotherhood of man striving along the way that makes all together, one with the Grand Architect.

The Redman did not worship the beast, but that part of the great one which he thought he saw under its form. Of all the animal kingdom, the serpent and the bird take the first place; especially the rattlesnake and eagle. In the estufa, or lodge room of the Moqui Indians, a bench runs around its three sides and on the fourth or north side it widens into a platform. On the east wall is generally a prayer in symbols, showing three rows of clouds in red and blue, from which hang black and white strips meant for rain, while from the left to right are long red and blue snakes meant for lightning. This prayer is to Omaia, God of the clouds, to send refreshing rains upon the Moqui crops. Instead of this, we place the letter G in the east. Space forbids my telling the interesting story of the snake dances. The eagle is revered because of his majestic flight, the Indians believing the spirit will be able to rise like him. It is from the same idea that man imagines a winged human form which he calls angel.

The sun and moon were also revered by the Red men. The Hurons say the moon is mistress of the souls of the dead and destroys the living. If anyone calls this foolish, take note of our own words referring to the moon's influence, lunatic, moonstruck, etc., and the Mason does not hesitate to revere the moon by making it a lesser light to govern his own night. We all know the sun holds a prominent place in Masonry; so it has with all peoples of past ages, and among the Indians. The Choctaws call fire *Shahli miko*, "the greatest chief," and speak of it as *Hashe Ittiapa*, "he who occupies the sun and the sun him." The tribes of the northwest coast say the original raven, who lived before the sun was made, found it by accident and placed it in the heavens where it has been ever since. These rude ideas show the tribes did not regard the sun itself as the creator, and fire was a type of life among them. The Algonquins said, "Their fire burns forever," when they spoke of the gods.

The Indians had indecent religious ceremonies, and, as collectors well know, many myths and stories told about the camp fire must be carefully censored before printing. Do not condemn the Indian for this, because he may well answer that the speaking leaves we call our Great Light have many things which are never read and never should be read to the people, and some are censored in the translation. For example, we are told that Abraham had his servant take an oath by placing his hand under his thigh, which was plainly on the phallic organ. Jacob also required such an oath. It is true we very properly aim for decency in our ceremonies, but we are not consistent at all times. We look unfavorably upon the Indian and his bluntness, in spite of these things in our holy writ. And also in spite of the fact that we have always had, since the oldest of us can remember, naughty boys among us who will, as naturally as a duck takes to water, chalk up certain organs upon fences and walls, which acts their elders frown severely upon, and at the same time we look at symbols of the same thing in churches, as quite a matter of course, because these signs as there shown are symbols and objects of religious veneration; so we carry them along, most of us not knowing really why. A commandment was once given, "Thou shalt not make unto thyself any graven image," yet the same book tells how Moses was ordered to make a brazen serpent for the people to look unto in order to be healed. Just the thing we look down upon the Indian for.

The Indians say we shall not forever die; even the grains of corn put under the earth grow up and become living things.

An old chief of the Creeks once said: "It is an old notion among us that when we die, the spirit goes the way the sun goes-to the west, and there joins its family and friends who went before." It is there, with general consent, the tribes north of Mexico supposed the happy hunting grounds to be. Masons, for the same reason, find the place of rest and payment of wages in the west.

Among the Comanches the body is buried at the sunsetting side of the camp, that the spirit may accompany the setting sun to the world beyond.

With the Dakotas the east stood for life and its source, so they lay a corpse with the head toward the east, to show a hope of future life. The Masonic grave is due east and west, but may there not be a mistake in the direction in which the body is commonly placed if we would faithfully carry out the same idea?

Our lodges, we are taught, are situated due east and west and a modem explanation is given of why this is so. Yet we find the Indian also made his council house or grand medicine lodge to extend east and west, and he does not give the same monitorial explanation as we do. The dead, whether it be the Indian or H. A., have been laid at all times in the track of the sun from east to west- toward that region where the sun sets, only to rise again in renewed brilliancy. The soul takes the same course, leaving the east in search of that which was lost, but like the divine star, ever traveling toward and with the rising sun.

A late work says, "Electricity is an invisible agent which manifests itself in various ways. The precise nature of electricity is unknown, but the effects produced by it, the method of controlling it and the laws governing its actions are becoming well known." Behold, here, science bow its head and whisper it does not know what this great power is, yet knows much about it. Let us fit the frame, to another truth. The soul is an invisible agent which manifests itself in various ways. The precise nature of the soul is unknown, but the effects produced by it, the methods of controlling it, and the laws governing its actions are becoming well known. Does it not fit perfectly? Among the Iroquois and Algonquins it was held that man has two souls, one of vegetative character, which gives him bodily life and remains with the corpse after death until it is called to enter another body; another soul of more ethereal texture, which in life can depart from the body in sleep or trance, and wander over the world, and at death goes directly to the land of spirits. This is the doctrine of the Theosophists. It cannot be said that the Indian ever acquired these ideas from Theosophists or was brought in contact with them so he would absorb them. He certainly put them forth from himself alone and it adds another argument in favor of the position that mind is but a single essence spread over the world.

A search for that which comes near to being an oath or obligation assumed, as it is practiced among the whites, has not been as well rewarded up to the present as might be wished, but, as it is due more to lack of time and of access to the right material, we may be able to supply something much more useful and interesting on this branch of our subject hereafter.

We have, however, something to say. There are no oaths or curses among the Sioux, or example, as we have them, but the Teton tribe can invoke the higher powers. Thus, one of them may say, "The Thunderers hear me"; "The Flying one really hears me." If he is lying, the Thunderers, or one of their number, will be sure to kill him. Sometimes the man will put a knife in his mouth, and then if he lies, he will be struck by a knife thereafter, and death must follow. Or he will say, "The horse heard me," knowing that the penalty for falsehood will be certain death from a horse that will throw him and break his neck. When one says, "The earth hears me," and he lies, he is sure to die miserably in a short time, and his family will also be afflicted.

Smet says, "The objects by which an Assiniboine swears are his gun, the skin of a rattlesnake, a bear's claw, and the wah-kon that the Indian interrogates. These various articles are placed before him and he says, 'In case my declarations prove false, may my gun fire and kill me, may the serpent bite me, may the bears tear and devour my flesh, and may my wah-kon overwhelm me with misery.' In extraordinary and very important affairs which demand formal promises, they call upon the Thunderer to witness their resolution to accomplish the acts proposed and accepted."

VI

THE NUMBER 4

In all religions a mystic power seems to have been attached to certain numbers. In the Hebrew Scripture the number 7 is said to occur over 360 times. The reason for the choice of numbers is not clear, but their sacred character appears to have begun when man first gave expression to a religious sentiment.

Masonry reveres numbers and so does the Indian, but only the number four stands out in this respect. We all remember how as children, simple as the savages, we were taught the points of the compass in school. If we stood with face to the rising sun, we would look toward the east, our backs would be to the west, our right hand to the south and our left to the north. The Redman, being a hunter, seems ever to have had these directions in mind and to have expressed himself accordingly of matters in his own house.

Travelers speak of one thing an Indian always does before serious business- to smoke. The old tradition has taught them to give the first puff to the sky, then one to each comer of the earth. Mr. Frush told me that the pipe filler passes the pipe to the old chief, who bows three times to the setting sun, and each times gives a puff toward the sun, raises the pipe and moves it aloft from west by the north to the east and then from the east by the south to the west again. We have a candidate start and go in these same directions. It originally and now means the same thing; so where is the great difference between some of their Masonry and ours? To the Indian, the spirits who made and governed the earth came from those points and are the leading figures in his tales and ceremonies. In the ceremonies of the *Mide-wiwin* of the Ojibwa, there are four degrees and these have different colored bands or stripes across the face for each degree. The Mason differs only in the objects he uses, for he has pins, or charms, or an apron, with which to ornament himself for the same reason his red brother paints his face. When the Chippewas initiated a candidate in *Meda* craft, he went to a lodge of four poles, with four stones before its fire, to remain four days and attend four feasts.

The burial ceremony as witnessed among the Otoe and Missouri Indians likewise sheds some light upon their beliefs and ceremonies. Upon burying a corpse they keep a fire at the grave four days and four nights. There is an ancient tradition that at the expiration of this time the Indian arose and mounting his spirit pony galloped away to the happy hunting grounds beyond. The Scriptures say, "Four days and four nights should the fires burn."

Among the Zuni Indians it is believed that the ghost hovers about the village four nights after death and starts on its journey to Kothluwalawa, (abiding place of the Council of the Gods), on the fifth morning. During the spirit's stay in the village the door and hatchway of the house must be left ajar that it may pass in and out at will. Should the door be closed, the ghost would scratch upon it and not be satisfied until it was opened. These shadow beings can be observed by seers and by others under certain conditions. No doubt the Zuni in saying this refer to those ecstatic or dream states already dwelt upon in a previous chapter.

At every step this number four or its multiple was repeated. It is but the same veneration of the cardinal points of the compass. In Masonry we are told there are four cardinal virtues instead of wind gods, for there is no other reason whatever why we should list off four instead of 3, 9, 13 or any other number. Be then also reminded, brother Masons, that in the same Great Light yonder on your altars the prophet Ezekiel says of the dry bones in the valley: "Then he said unto me, prophesy unto the wind, prophesy son of man and say to the wind;... come from the four winds O breath, arid breathe upon these slain that they may live." And again it is said that the ashes of certain persons shall be scattered to the four winds of heaven! Why not have simply said, to the winds which around us may blow? Thus I make it plain to you that in the number four and in scattering ashes to the four winds, an important part of Masonry, supported by what we are told to take as our rule and guide of faith, is exactly in common with what the despised Indian believes.

The great spirit of the dead lives in the dark north is the tradition among the Ottawas, and there the Mason finds his place of darkness, about which is woven a legend of fancy, probably far from the real origin.

When about to go to war, the Cherokee Shaman or Medicine man stands behind the warriors, who face the east at the edge of a stream, looking down upon the water, while the Shaman repeats the war-song or prayer. This is done for four successive nights, just before setting out. He puts the souls of the doomed enemy in the lower regions, where the black war clubs are constantly warring about, and envelopes them in a black fog which shall never be lifted, and out of which they shall never reappear. The souls of the Shaman's friends are to be raised to the seventh heaven, where they shall go about in peace, shielded by the red war club of success, never to be knocked about by the enemy.

To break the soul in two means to cut the thread of life, they believing the soul to be an intangible something having length like a stick or string.

Red, symbolic of success, is the color of the war club; black typical of death. Blue is emblematic of failure, disappointment, or unsatisfied desire. The blue spirits live in the north. They shall never become blue, means they shall succeed. To pray that another become blue, is to pray for his failure. White denotes peace and happiness, and was the color of the pipe anciently used in peace treaties. The white spirits live in the south.

And thus again we see that the white man who "has the blues" still keeps the same old superstition the Indian received from his forefathers. We do not use colors symbolically in all ways as the Indians did, but we agree with him that black stands for death and white for peace.

Following is a translation of the Cherokee prayer which will thus be better understood with this short explanation and no doubt will be interesting:

"Hayi! Yu! Listen! Now quickly we have lifted up the red war club. Quickly his soul shall be without motion. There under the earth, where the black war clubs shall be moving about like ball sticks in the game, there his soul shall be, never to reappear. We cause It to be so. He shall never go and lift up the war club. We cause it to be so. There under the earth the black war club and the black fog have come together as one for their covering. It shall never move about (i. e., the black fog shall never be lifted from them). We cause it to be so. Instantly their souls shall be moving about there in the seventh heaven. Their souls shall never break in two. So let it be. Quickly we have moved them (their souls) on high for them, where they shall be going about in peace. You have shielded yourselves with the red war club. Their souls shall never be knocked about. Cause it to be so. There on high their souls shall be going about. Let them shield themselves with the red war club. Quickly grant that they shall never become blue. Yu!"

On Nov. 4, 1906, the Jesuits held their "Quadrivium" for the purpose of electing a General of their order to succeed the late Father Martin. According to their rules, they hold a four days' session, when they are locked up from the world in secret conclave. Naturally will again occur to us the question, Why do they hold a session of just four instead of some other number of days? It must be answered in no other way than that of a continuation of old pagan traditions. Neither Mason nor Jesuit can with honesty defeat the sound records of history, when they oppose it with legend and tradition. The Indian does not seek to do so.

When the rainmaker of the Lenni Lenape would exert his power, he retired to some secluded spot and drew upon the earth the figure of a cross, its arms toward the cardinal points, placed upon it a piece of tobacco, a gourd, a bit of some red stuff, and commenced to cry aloud to the spirits of the rains. The Creeks, at the festival of the Busk, celebrated to the four winds, and according to their legends instituted by them, commenced by making the new fire. The manner of this was to place four logs in the center of a square end to end, forming a cross, the outer ends pointing to the cardinal points and in the center of the new cross the new fire was made. The Busk was a grand commemorative festival of the Creeks, which wiped out the memory of all crimes but murder, and which reconciled the proscribed criminal to his nation and atoned for his guilt. When the green corn was served up, every dance, every invocation, every ceremony was shaped and ruled by the application of the number four and its multiples in every imaginable relation.

In the snake dance of the Moqui Indians they use four kinds of "medicine," being four kinds of roots. Consideration of the number four leads me naturally to a symbol which for all ages has fascinated the human mind. For some unknown reason it does not appear as a symbol in the first three Masonic degrees, and therein the Indian has gone further. Scholars have offered many different and often vulgar, debasing interpretations of the cross. With the Indian, it was a nobler emblem, and the Catholics found it here when they discovered the country. The arms pointed to the cardinal points and represented the four winds, the rain bringers.

INDIAN MASONRY

Of the many forms of the cross, the swastika is the most ancient. Notwithstanding the theories and speculations of scholars, its origin is really unknown. This symbol has been found in all parts of the world.

WAR SHIELD, PIMA INDIANS.- OGEE SWASTIKA OF THREE COLORS, BLUE, RED, AND WHITE- US NATIONAL MUSEUM (Cat. No. 27829)

It came into being before history, and it may properly be classed as prehistoric, so ancient it is.

The swastika, svastika, or suastika, the first form being now generally accepted as the English spelling, is thus defined in Littre's French Dictionary: "A mystic figure used by several East Indian sects. It was equally well known to the Brahmins and Buddhists. Most of the rock inscriptions in the Buddhist caverns in the west of India are preceded or followed by the holy sign of the swastika. It is a Sanskrit word meaning happiness, pleasure, good luck. It is composed of *su,* 'good,' and *asti,* 'being,' or 'good being,' with suffix *ka.*"

The writer is inclined to think this author has narrowed the origin and name of the swastika by assigning it apparently only to India, and retaining the name given it there.

The symbol is a monogrammatic sign of four branches, of which the ends are curved or bent at right angles, and two forms of it are seen in the illustrations accompanying these pages. Many theories have been presented concerning the symbolism of the swastika, its relation to ancient deities, and its representation of certain qualities. Some writers declare it to be a symbol of the phallic religion, and it has been held to stand for many a different god. Whatever else the sign stood for, and however many meanings it may have had, it was always ornamental. I have seen it worn in our day by women and girls, who certainly did not know what it was, thus clearly using it simply for ornament, as a design of pleasing and curious form, and no doubt it was so used anciently. I am inclined to the belief that in spite of its many interpretations, it is nothing more than a form of the cross with crampons, and as a cross, pointed to the four cardinal points as explained further along. This is said because of the fact that it was found with our Indians, and the writer believes they never obtained it from the white man, but always had it. The common form of cross, the Maltese cross, and the swastika are all to be seen in the illustrations herein, comprising a war shield, sand painting of the Navajoes, mantle and medicine shirt of the Apache Indians, as also a ghost shirt of the Arapahoes. In all of these we may find much detail of great interest. It will be particularly noted in the Navajo sand painting, that four gods are represented at the four points of the compass, and these figures form a cross as well as having the swastika near each. Between them are different plants. The Indians of the southwest, who lived in fixed abodes, have elaborated their religious system far more in pictographic detail than the nomadic tribes of the north. These latter, however, as will be seen from the designs, used and had the same signs, whatever they stood for, thus again proving the unity of man, in conceiving the same idea of a pictographic or constructed form reduced to permanency.

The Blackfeet arranged glacial stones on the prairies in the form of a cross, in honor, they said, of Natose, "the old man who sends the winds." As an emblem of the winds which send the fertilizing showers, it is above all- the tree of our life, our nourishment, our health. It never had any other meaning in America. In Mexican the cross was properly called *Tonacaquahuitl*, or tree of our life- of our flesh. Most nations have revered some shrub or growing thing. The Egyptians revered the lotus and the Mason the acacia. The Indian revered his ghost tree. It is the sign of life and the visible symbol of that which our ancestors adored.

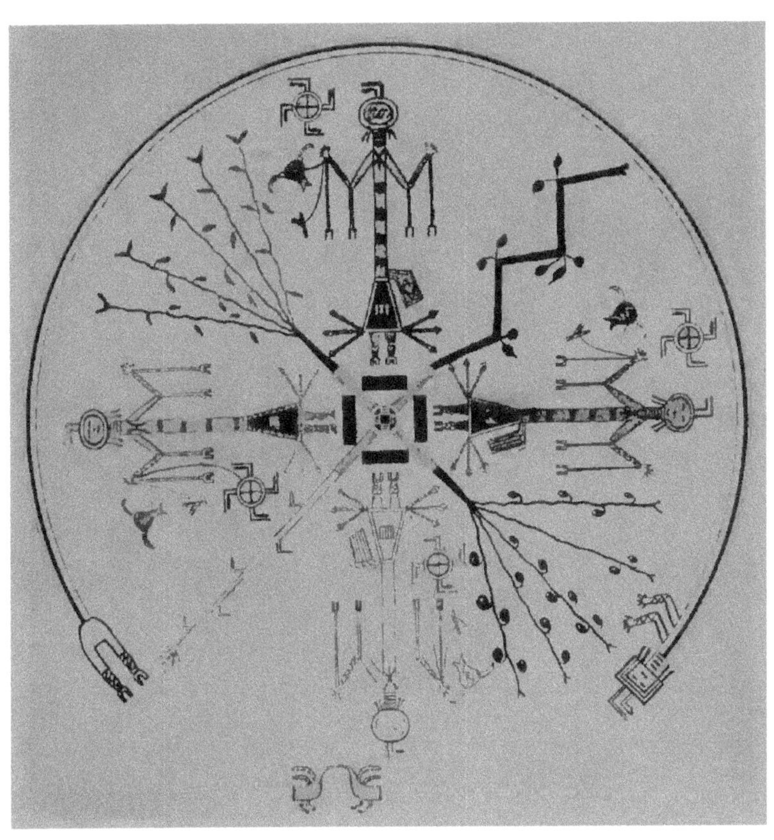

NAVAJO INDIAN SAND PAINTING (VIEWED FROM THE EAST.) -REPORT BUREAU, AMERICAN ETHNOLOGY, VOL V. PAGE 450.

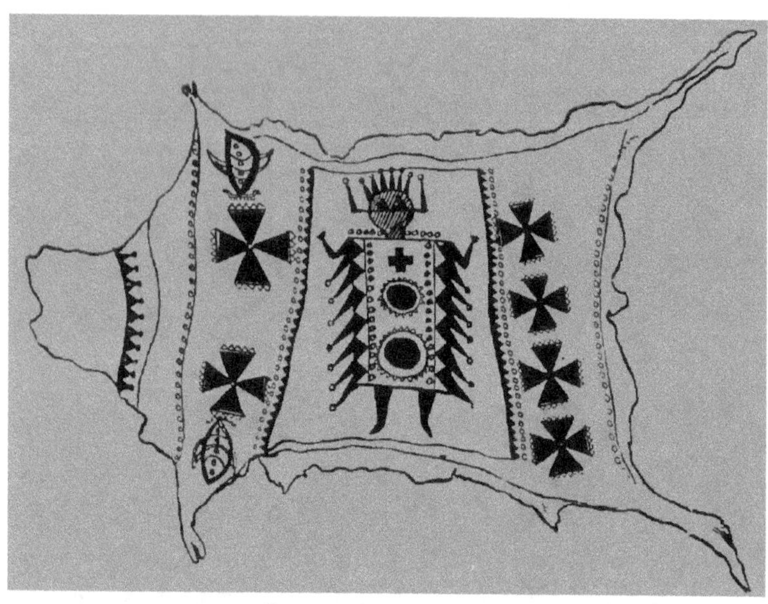

MANTLE OF INVISIBILITY. APACHE INDIANS. -REPORT
BUREAU AMERICAN ETHNOLOGY, VOL. X, PAGE 504.

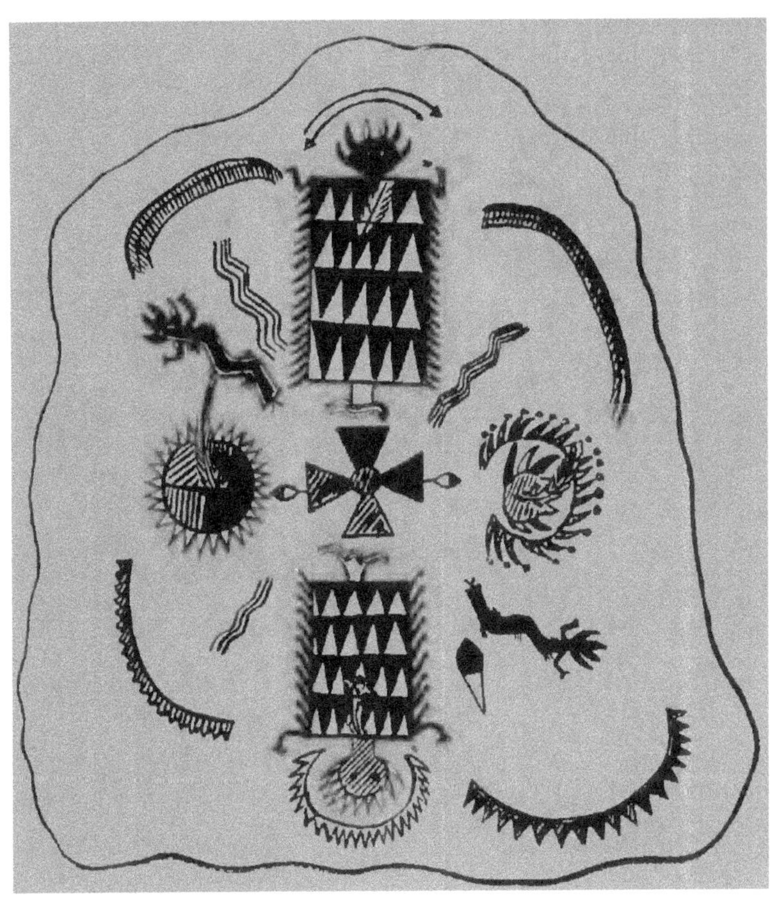

MEDICINE SHIRT, APACHE INDIANS. -REPORT BUREAU AMERICAN ETHNOLOGY, VOL. IX, PAGE 590.

GHOST SHIRT, ARAPAHO INDIANS. -REPORT BUREAU
AMERICAN ETHNOLOGY. PART 2, PAGE 895.

VII

OJIBWA GRAND MEDICINE LODGE

The following two chapters of this book will be devoted to a consideration of the Grand Medicine Lodge of the Ojibwa Indians. Many years ago a treaty was made with these Indians by the United States Government, by which they relinquished about 4,000,000 acres of land and moved to the Red Lake and White Earth Reservations, where they took lands in severally, and, under the treaty, became citizens and lost their tribal government. The chief Mide priests were well aware of this momentous change and its consequences, and foreseeing that such a change of habits would follow among their people that they could no longer continue the ceremonies of the so-called "pagan rites," they were persuaded and became willing to impart them to Dr. W. J. Hoffman, in order that a complete description might be made and preserved for the future information of their descendants. Dr. Hoffman was the duly authorized representative of the Bureau of Ethnology of the government and performed his task with the greatest fidelity as his account in these pages will clearly show. It is barely possible that there are a few very old Indians who even at this late day try secretly to perform some of the old ceremonies, but beyond such feeble attempts, the ancient glory of the Midewiwin is now but a tradition.

I have spread out on these pages practically most of the detail, although by no means all of it, for the reason that I am sure a more perfect picture of the forms and ceremonies practiced will show wherein the Redman and the paleface have followed trails which ever and anon do approach each other, not only in speaking, but in touching distance, as they travel onward toward the same goal. These things will bear out the deductions I have made and to which attention has been called. The wisdom of giving the most accurate information will be seen when an examination of

INDIAN MASONRY

Mackey's Encyclopedia of Freemasonry shows that he fell into error under his title "American Mysteries," where, relying on Brinton, he says the Indians had three degrees or grades, the Waubeno, the Meda, and the Jossakeed, the last being the highest. This is clearly wrong, as I shall now show. There is no doubt that the careful reader will turn over the material I have here prepared for him and, looking at it from other viewpoints than those from which I may have particularly directed his attention, will behold the intensely interesting and wonderful field before him in these "pagan rites." He will only regret with me that we are unable to get even closer to and into and pass down along that same trail the Redman trod, so we might see with his eyes what was there; but alas, all those trails the Ojibwa followed have become dim and the blazes overgrown with the bark and moss of many winters.

Investigations among a number of tribes of the Algonquian linguistic division shows that the traditions and practices pertaining to the Midewiwin, Society of the Mide or Shamans, popularly designated as the "Grand Medicine Society," prevailed generally, and the rites may still be practiced at irregular intervals, though in slightly different forms in various localities Jessakkid and the Midewiwin and it is seldom, if at all, that a Mide becomes a Jessakkid, although the latter sometimes gains admission into the Midewiwin, chiefly with the intention of strengthening his power with his tribe.

The origin of the Midewiwin or Mide Society, commonly called the Grand Medicine Society, although erroneously, is buried in obscurity. The Mide in the true sense of the word is a Shaman, although various authors have called him powwow, medicine man, priest, seer, prophet, etc. A number of years ago, W. W. Warren, a mixed-blood Ojibwa and a well educated man, began a history which would have been exceedingly valuable had not his death interrupted its completion. In his writings he said that the Me-da-we rite has incorporated in it most of the ancient traditions among the Ojibwas- songs and traditions that have descended not orally, but in hieroglyphics, for at least a long time of generations. In this rite is also perpetuated the purest and most ancient idioms of the language, which differs somewhat from that of common everyday use. He also says that this ancient custom of Me-da-we is still shrouded in mystery even to his own eyes, although he had the great advantage of thoroughly understanding their language, a relationship with them, and especially their confidence and friendship.

The Ojibwas believe in a multiplicity of spirits or Manidos which inhabit all space, and every conspicuous object in nature. These Manidos in turn are subservient to superior ones, either of a charitable or benevolent character, or those who are malignant and aggressive. The chief or superior Manido is termed Kitshi Manido-Great Spirit- approaching to a great extent the idea of our God of the Christian religion. The second in their estimation is Dzhe Manido, a benign being, upon whom they look as the guardian spirit of the Midewiwin and through whose divine provision the sacred rites of the Mide were granted to man. The Animiki or Thunder-god is, if not the supreme, at least one of the greatest of the malignant Manidos, and it is from him that the Jessakkid are believed to obtain the powers of evil doing. There is one other who abides in and rules the "Place of Shadows," the hereafter. He is known as Dzhibai Manido, "Shadow Spirit," or more commonly Ghost Spirit. The name of Kitshi Manido is never mentioned but with reverence and thus only in connection with the rite of Mide or a sacred feast, and always after making an offering of tobacco.

The first important event in the life of an Ojibwa youth is his first fast. He goes to a secluded spot in the forest and fasts for an indefinite number of days, and when reduced by abstinence from food, he enters a hysterical or ecstatic state, in which he may have visions or hallucinations. The objects they most desire to see are mammals and birds, though any object, animate or inanimate, is considered a good omen. The object which first appears is adopted as the personal mystery, guardian spirit or tutelary demon for him, and is never mentioned without first making a sacrifice. The future course of the faster is governed by his dream and if he thinks he beheld some powerful Manido, or other object held in reverence by the Mide Society, he may have a desire to join it. Whether he. is impelled by a dream or any other motive, the applicant takes the same course. He applies to a prominent Mide priest for advice.

The priest, if favorable, consults his companions and action is taken, the question of preliminary instructions, fees, presents, etc., being formally talked over. If all is agreed upon, an instructor or preceptor is designated, to whom the applicant must go and make an agreement as to the amount of preparatory information to be gained, as well as for the fees and other presents to be given in return. These presents have nothing to do with the presents which must be presented to the Mide priests before his initiation, the latter being gathered up during the time that is devoted to preliminary instruction, which usually lasts for several years. Thus plenty of time is found for hunting, as skins and pelts which are not required as presents may be exchanged for blankets, tobacco, kettles, guns, etc., from traders. Sometimes a long number of years are spent in preparation for the first degree of the Mide, and there are many who have impoverished themselves in the payment of fees and the preparation for the feast, to which all visiting priests are also invited.

The Midewiwin consists of an indefinite number of Mide of both sexes. The society is graded into four separate and distinct degrees, although there is a general impression among certain members that any degree beyond the first is only a mere repetition. The greater power attained by one in making advancement depends upon the fact of his having submitted to "being shot at with the medicine sacks," in the hands of the officiating priests. This may be the case in these latter days in certain localities, but investigation shows that there is considerable variation in the dramatization of the ritual. One circumstance stands out to the careful observer and that is the greater the number of repetitions of the phrases chanted by the Mide, the greater is felt to be the amount of inspiration and power of the performance. This is also true of the lectures of some of them, in which the reiteration and prolongation in time of delivery helps very much to lastingly impress the candidate and other onlookers with the importance and sacredness of the ceremony.

It has always been the custom of the Mide priests to preserve birch bark records bearing delicate incised lines to represent pictorially the ground plan of the number of degrees to which the owner is entitled. Such records and charts are sacred and never exposed to the public view, being brought forward for inspection only when an accepted candidate has paid his fees, and then only after necessary preparation by fasting and offerings of tobacco.

During 1887 at Red Lake, Minn., Dr. Hoffman had the good fortune to discover an old birch bark chart and to secure inspection of the drawings and photograph it. It measured seven feet, one and one-half inches by eighteen inches and was. made of five pieces of birch bark neatly and securely stitched together by means of thin, flat strands of basswood. At each end are two thin strips of wood secured transversely by wrapping and stitching with thin strands of bark, so as to prevent splitting and fraying the ends of the record. This chart gives the tradition of Mi-nabozho, the servant of Dzhe Manido, and the origin of the Midewiwin. It is admitted by all Mide priests that much of the information has been lost through the death of their aged predecessors and they feel convinced that at last all the sacred character of the work will be forgotten or lost through the adoption of new religions by the young people, and the death of the Mide priests, who refuse to accept Christianity and are in consequence termed pagans.

Initiation of later years was performed during the latter part of the summer. The ceremonies were performed in public. The ritual was unintelligible to those not initiated and the important part of the necessary information is given to the candidate in a preceptor's wigwam. The Mide-wigan or Mide-wigiwam, or Grand Medicine Lodge, commonly called, is usually built in an open grove or clearing. It measures about eighty by twenty feet and extends east and west, the main entrance being toward that point of the compass at which the sun rises. The walls are made of poles and saplings eight to ten feet high, planted firmly in the ground and wattled with short branches and twigs having leaves. In the east and west walls are open spaces about four feet wide used as entrances. From each side of the opening, walls extend at right angles so as to make a short hallway leading in. Branches are laid over the top for shade. About ten feet from the east or main entrance, a large flat stone of over a foot in diameter is placed upon the ground. About ten feet from the western entrance is planted a sacred Mide post or cedar, that for the first degree being about seven feet high and six or eight inches thick. It is painted red with a band of green four inches wide around the top. Upon the top is fixed the stuffed body of an owl. Midway between the stone and post on the floor is spread a blanket upon which the gifts and presents are afterwards deposited. A short distance from each of the outer angles of the structure are planted cedar or pine trees, each about ten feet in height. About one hundred yards east of the main entrance is built a wigiwam or sweat lodge to be used by the candidate, both to take his vapor baths and to receive final instructions from his preceptor. This wigiwam is dome-shaped and measures about ten feet in diameter.

FIRST DEGREE

At each meeting of the candidate he receives only a limited amount of instruction from his instructor, who hopes for greater fees and also that he may be looked upon with greater awe and reverence. For these reasons he gives most of his information in very ambiguous form. The peculiar properties of the drum, rattle, migis, etc., and their powers in exorcising evil spirits and curing the sick are explained. The candidate is also instructed in the Mide songs and prepares his chart with mnemonic characters for his songs. He also has instruction in the properties of herbs and plants. He may be taken into the woods at times, where a certain plant or tree is found, which is approached, a smoke offering made before it or other object sought, a small pinch of tobacco put into the hole from which it is taken. This is an offering to Noko-mis, the earth, the grandmother of mankind, for the benefits which are derived from her body, where they were placed by Kitshi Manido. Of later years the third and fourth degrees were seldom conferred, not only because of the cost being beyond the reach of a candidate, but because of the opposition of missionaries and Indian agents, who looked upon all these ceremonies as a hindrance to the progress of Christianity or educational influences.

When the preparatory instruction is ended and a day set for the initiation, the preceptor sings to his pupil a song extolling his own efforts and the high virtues of the knowledge imparted. About ten days or two weeks before the day of initiation, the chief Mide priest sends out to all the members invitations which consist of sticks or twigs about one-fourth inch thick and six or seven inches long. The runner is charged with giving the person invited full information of the day of ceremony and the place. Sometimes the sticks have bands of color painted around one end, usually green but sometimes red, though both colors may be employed, the two ends being thus tinted. The person thus invited is obliged to bring with him his invitation stick, and upon entering the Mide-wigan he lays it upon the ground near the sacred stone, on the side toward the degree post. In case a Mide is unable to attend he sends his invitation with a statement of the reason why. The number of sticks upon the floor is counted on the morning of the day of initiation and the number of those present to attend the ceremonies is known beforehand. About five or six days before the day set for the ceremony, the candidate moves to the neighborhood of the Mide-wigan. On the eve of the fifth day he goes to the sudatory or sweat lodge. When seated within, he is given water, which he pours on heated stones placed there by assistants, and vapor is caused to form, by means of which he perspires. This act of purification is absolutely necessary and must be performed once each day for four days, though the process may be shortened by taking two vapor baths in one day, thus limiting the process to two days. This however is permitted or desired only under extraordinary circumstances. During the process of purgation the candidate's thoughts must dwell upon the seriousness of the course he is pursuing and the sacred character of the new life he is about to assume. When fumigation has ceased, he is visited by the preceptor and the other officiating Mide priests, when the talk is confined chiefly to the candidate's progress. He then gives each a present of tobacco, and after offering to Kitshi Manido with the pipe, they expose the articles contained in their Mide sacks and explain and expatiate upon the merits and properties of each of the magical objects. The candidate for the first time learns of the manner of preparing effigies, etc., with which to present to the incredulous ocular demonstrations of the genuineness and divine origin of the Mide-wiwin, or as it is in this connection termed, a religion. Several methods are employed for the purpose and the greater the power of the Mide, the greater will appear the mystery connected with the exhibition. This may be performed whenever circumstances demand such proof, but the tests are made before the candidate with a two-fold purpose; first, to impress him with the supernatural powers of the Mide themselves, and second, in an oracular manner to ascertain if Kitshi Manido is pleased with the ceremony about to take place and with the initiation of that candidate. The first test is made by laying on the floor of the wigiwam a string of four wooden beads about an inch in diameter. After the owner of these has chanted for a few moments in an almost inaudible voice, the beads begin to roll from side to side as if animated. The string is then quickly put back in the Mide sack. One of the most astonishing tests and one that can be produced only by a Mide of the highest power, is that of causing a Mide sack to move on the ground as if alive. It is quite probable some small animal may be placed within the sack to do this trick or it may be otherwise performed. In most of the private exhibitions the light is dim so as to prevent deception being found out and made known. When the demonstrations are public, the auditors invariably consist of the most credulous of the initiated, or the associates of the performers, from whom no opposition is expected.

When the four vapor baths have been taken and the eve of ceremony arrives, the candidate remains in the sweat lodge longer than usual so as not to come in contact with visitors. The woods resound with noises incident to a large camp. In various directions may be heard monotonous beating of drums showing the presence of a number of dancers, or the hard, sharp taps of the Mide drum caused by a priest propitiating and invoking the presence and favor of Kitshi Manido in the ceremony near at hand. When the night is far advanced and all is still, the candidate, with only his instructor, goes to his own wigiwam. At daybreak, the candidate breakfasts and goes to the sweat lodge to await the coming of his preceptor and later the officiating priests. The candidate puts on his best clothing and such articles of beaded ornaments as he may possess. Preceptor and priests are also clad in their finest, each wearing one or two beaded dancing bags at his side, fastened by a band of beaded cloth, crossing the opposite shoulder. The members not directly concerned take seats about the wall of the Mide-wigan where they smoke or occasionally drum and sing. The drummer with his assistants takes a place near, upon the floor of the sacred enclosure, to the left of the eastern door, that is to say, the southeast corner.

If the day is dark or threatening, one of the priests accompanying the candidate, sings a song to dispel the clouds, of which these are some of the words:

I swing the spirit like a child.
The sky is what I am telling you about.
(That is, the sky and earth united by a pathway of possible

rain.)

We have lost the sky. (i. e., it becomes dark and the arm of the Mide is reaching up into it for its favor of clear weather.)

I am helping you. (The otter-skin Mide sack is held up to influence the Otter Spirit to aid them.)

I have made an error (in sending). (If the otter-skin Mide sack has failed in its mission.)

The Mide women who have gathered outside the lodge now begin to dance as the song is renewed.

I am using my heart. (Refers to sincerity of motives in practice of the Mide ceremony.)

What are you saying to me, and am I "in my senses"?

The spirit wolf. (One of the evil spirits who is opposed to having the ceremony is assisting the evil Manidos in causing the sky to be overcast.)

I do not know where I am going. (The Mide is in doubt whether to proceed or not with the initiation.)

I depend on the clear sky. (To have the ceremony go on.)

I give you the other village, spirit that you are. (That rain should fall anywhere but upon the gathering there in the Mide-wigan.)

The thunder is heavy.

We are talking to one another, (i. e., the Mide communes with Kitshi Manido.)

If the clouds disappear, or the sky is already clear, the candidate goes to his sweat lodge, where he is joined by his preceptor and later by the priests. After all preliminaries are arranged, the preceptor sings a song:

The spirit man is crying out,
Talking around in various places.
The spirit is flying.
The day is clear; let us have the grand medicine.
I am the sign that the day will be clear.
I am the strongest medicine, is what he said of me.

The spirit in the middle of the sky sees me.
I take my sack and touch him.
My medicine is the sacred spirit.
How do you answer me, my Mide friends?

This is an inquiry as to whether the priests are willing to proceed. Upon the song ending, there is a brief pause and all partake of a smoke in perfect silence, making the usual offerings by presenting the pipe to the four points of the compass, upward to Kitshi Manido and downward to No-komis or mother earth. The preceptor then says:

Now is the time; he hears us:
All of us, the one who made the Midewiwin.
After this he addresses the candidate in the Mide gagi-kwewin or Mide sermon as follows:
Now listen to me what I am about to say to you.
If you take heed of that which I say to you, so shall continue always your life.
Now today I make known to you the Great Spirit, that which he says, and now this I say to you:
This is what says the Great Spirit, that he loves you.
It shall be white, the sacred objects at the time when they shall let it be known, and this is what I say.
That which he says the Great Spirit, now this I Impart to you, even if they say that they saw me dead; in this he shall be place.
Raised again, in this place he puts his trust.
In my heart, in this "saying," the time of duration of the world.
It shall never fail.
That is what he says, the Spirit.
My child this shall give you life.

The Mide priests then leave the sweat lodge and wait for the candidate, who gathers up in his arms small presents like tobacco, handkerchiefs, etc.

The line of march is then formed, with the candidate first, then his preceptor, followed by the officiating priests, then such others, members of the family, relatives and so on, as may desire. At the door of the Mide-wigan all but one of the priests continue and take stations inside, the preceptor remaining at the side of the candidate, the Mide priest on the other side of him. Then the candidate and all with him march four times around the outside of the enclosure toward the left or south, during which time drumming is continued within. Upon completion of the fourth circuit the candidate is placed so as to face the main entrance of the Mide-wigan. He is prompted to say, "Let me come in and these I put down; my things" (gifts). The presents are then laid upon the ground. The preceptor goes inside, taking with him the gifts deposited by the candidate and remains standing just inside the door and faces the degree post toward the west. Then the officiating priest, who has remained at the side of the candidate turns toward the latter and in a clear, distinct, and exceedingly impressive manner sings the following chant addressed to Kitshi Manido, whose invisible form is supposed to abide within the Mide-wigan during such ceremonies, and which states that the candidate is presented to receive life (migis) for which he is suffering, and invoking the divine favor.

> There is a spirit, ho
> Just as the one above, he.
> Now sits with me my child and now I proclaim, he, hwe.
> That I enter you here, my father good spirit, ho, hwe.
> Have pity on me, he, hwe,
> Now that I enter him here,
> He that is suffering for life,
> Believe me that he shall live,
> My father, whose child I am, he, he.

The candidate is then led within the enclosure, when all

the members of the society arise while he is slowly led around toward the southern side to the extreme end in the west, thence toward the right and back along the western side to the point of beginning. This is done four times. As he starts upon his march, the member nearest the door falls in the line of procession, each member continuing to drop in at the rear, until the entire assembly is in motion. During this movement there is a monotonous drumming upon the Mide drums and the chief Mide priest sings:

I go through (the) "house" the long. (i. e., through the Mide-wigan).

At the fourth circuit the members begin to stop at the places previously occupied by them, the candidate going on, and remaining with his preceptor, to a point just inside the eastern entrance, while the four officiating priests continue around toward the opposite end of the enclosure and station themselves in a semi-circle just beyond the degree post and facing the western door. Upon the ground before them are spread blankets and similar goods which have been removed from the beams above, and upon which the candidate is to kneel. He is then led to the western extremity of the enclosure, where he stands upon the blankets spread upon the ground, and faces the four Mide priests. The preceptor takes his position behind and a little to one side of the candidate, another assistant being called upon by the preceptor to occupy a corresponding position upon the other side. During this procedure there is a gentle drumming which ceases after all have been properly stationed. The preceptor then steps to a point to the side and front of the candidate, and near the officiating priests and says: "The time has now arrived that I yield it to you (the Mide-migis), that will give you life." The preceptor then returns to his position back of and a little to one side of the candidate, when the chief officiating priest sings the following song, accompanying upon a small Mide drum:

You shall hear me, spirit that you are.

After the song is ended the drum is handed to one of the members sitting near by, when the fourth and last of the officiating priests says to the candidate, who is now placed on his knees, "Now is the time that I hope of you, that you shall take life, the bead (migis shell)." The priest then grasps his Mide-sack as if holding a gun, and, clutching it near the top with the left hand extended, while with the right he clutches it below the middle or near the base, he aims it toward the candidate's left breast and makes a thrust forward toward the target, uttering the syllables, "Ya, ho, ho, ho, ho, ho," rapidly rising to a higher key. He recovers his first position and repeats the movement three times, becoming more and more animated, the last time making a vigorous gesture toward the kneeling man's breast as if shooting him. While this is going on the preceptor and his assistants place their hands upon the candidate's shoulders and cause his body to tremble. Then the third and second Mide go through similar movements, the candidate being caused to agitate himself more violently. The chief priest now places himself in a threatening attitude and says to the Mide: "Mi'-dzhi-de-a-mi-shik', put your helping heart with me," and imitating the others as already described. After repeating the syllables the fourth time, he aims the Mide-sack at the candidate's head, and as the migis is supposed to be shot into it, he falls forward upon the ground apparently lifeless. Then the four Mide priests, the preceptor and assistants lay their Mide-sacks upon his back, and after a few moments a migis shell drops from his mouth, where he had been instructed to retain it. The chief Mide picks up the migis and holding it between the thumb and index finger of the right hand, extending his arm toward the candidate's mouth, says, "Wa! wa! he, he, he, he," the last syllable being uttered in a high key, and rapidly dropped to a low note. Then the same words are uttered while the migis is held toward the east, and in regular succession to the south, west, north, and toward the sky. During this time the candidate has begun to partially revive and get upon his knees, but when the Mide finally places the migis in his mouth again, he instantly falls upon the ground as before. The Mide then take up the sacks, each grasping his own as before and as they pass around the inanimate body they touch it at various points, which causes the candidate to "return to life." The chief priest then says to him, "O'mishgan," get up- which he does; then indicating to the holder of the Mide drum to bring that to him, he begins tapping, and presently sings a song, repeating the sentence.

> This is what I am, my fellow Mide;
> I fear all my fellow Mide.

At the conclusion of the song the preceptor prompts the candidate to ask the chief Mide, "Colleague, instruct me, give me a song." In response the Mide teaches him the following, uttered as a monotonous chant:

> What are you asking, grand medicine, are you asking?

> I will give you, you want me to give you grand medicine.

> Always take care of; you have received it yourself, never forget.

The candidate replies, "Yes, thanks for giving me, to me life." Then the priests begin to look around in search of places to sit, saying, "Now is the time I look around where we shall be (sit)," and all go to the places reserved or made for them.

The new member then goes to the pile of blankets and other gifts and divides them among the four officiating priests, reserving some of less value for the preceptor and his assistant, while tobacco is carried around to each person present. All then make an offering of smoke, to the east, south, west, north, toward the center and top of the Mide-wigan- where Kitshi Manido presides- and to the earth. Then each person blows smoke upon his or her Mide-sack as an offering to the sacred migis within. The chief Mide advances to the new member and presents him with a new Mide-sack, made of otter skin, or perhaps the skin of a mink or weasel, after which he returns to his place. The new member rises, goes to the chief Mide, who bends his head forward, and passing both flat hands down over either side of the head of the latter, says:

"Thanks, my colleagues, my colleagues, my colleagues." Then approaching all others according to their rank, he does the same thing.

At the conclusion of this ceremony, the new Mide returns to his place, and after putting his migis into his own Mide-sack, he goes to the person sitting nearest the eastern entrance on the south side and tests his own powers by shooting the sack as was done in his own case until he has them all apparently rendered unconscious by the powerful effects of the migis, and the same thing is gone through with as in his own case, all finally recovering.

After this another curious ceremony takes place. Each one places his migis shell upon his right palm, the Mide-sack being held with the left hand, and, moving around the enclosure, shows his migis to everyone present, saying constantly in a quick, low tone, "Ho, ho, ho, ho." During this time all present mingle together, each striving to get the attention of the others. Each Mide pretends to swallow his migis, when suddenly there are sounds of violent coughing, as if the actors were strangling, and soon thereafter they gag and spit the migis out upon the ground, then each falls as though dead. In a few moments however, they recover, take up the little shells again and pretend to swallow them. As the Mide return to their respective places the migis is restored to its place in the Mide- sack. Food is then brought into the Mide-wigan and all partake of it at the expense of the new member.

After the feast, the older Mide of high order, and possibly the officiating priests, recount the traditions of the Anishinabeg and the origin of the Midewiwin, together with sacred speeches relating to the benefits to be derived through a knowledge thereof, and sometimes tales of individual success and exploits. After all this, the new member is called upon to give evidence of his skill as a singer and a Mide, so he has under the counsel of his preceptor composed a song and borrowing a drum, he sings it for them. Much depends upon his success in this respect to gain friends and those who will speak well of him.

As the sun approaches the western horizon, the Mide priests go out of the western door of the Mide- wigan to their respective wigiwams, where they take their regular evening meal, after which the evening is spent in paying calls upon other members of the society, smoking, etc.

The preceptor and his assistant return to the Mide-wigan at nightfall, remove the degree post and plant it at the head of the wigiwam- that part directly opposite the entrance- occupied by the new member. Two stones are placed at the base of the post, to represent the two forefeet of the bear Manido through whom life was also given to the Ani-shina'beg.

If there should be more than one candidate, the whole number, if not too great, is taken into the Mide-wigan for initiation at the same time; and if one day suffices to do the business for which the meeting was called, the Indians return to their respective homes upon the following morning. If, however, it has been arranged to give a member a higher degree, the necessary changes and arrangements of the Mide-wigan are begun at once after the society adjourns.

In the Mide-sacks are carried the sacred objects belonging to the owner, such as colors for the face, the magic red powder, used in the preparation of the hunters' songs; effigies and other contrivances to prove to the incredulous the genuineness of the Mide pretensions, sacred songs, amulets, and other small

INDIAN MASONRY

Manidos- trinkets to which they attach supernatural properties- invitation twigs, etc.

The female Mide is usually present at the initiation of new members, but her duties are mainly to assist in the singing and to make herself generally useful in connection with the preparation of the medicine feast.

SECOND DEGREE

The arrangement of the Mide-wigan for the second degree is very much like that for the first, the only important difference being that there are two degree posts instead of one. The first post is set a short distance beyond the middle of the floor, toward the western door, and is similar to the first degree post, that is, red with a band of green around the top, upon which is perched the stuffed body of an owl. The second post of similar size is painted red and over its entire surface are spots of white. These spots are symbolical of the sacred migis, the number of them denoting increased power of the magic influence which fills the Mide-wigan. The sweat lodge, as before, is erected some distance east of the main entrance but is larger so as to permit more occupants, as it requires a larger number of Mide priests for the preparation and instruction of the candidate.

The candidate is now aware of the course he must take when he seeks advancement. Before making his application, he must make presents and gifts of twice the value for the first degree, and as the hunting seasons do not enable him to get these things so soon it is generally a year or more before he can proceed. When he is ready, he invites eight of the Mide who have the higher degree to his wigiwam and tells them he wishes to present himself for initiation at the proper time. A feast is set before them, tobacco is presented and smoking indulged in for the purpose of making proper offerings as already described.

If the priests are satisfied with the gifts and favorable to the candidate, he secures the services of one of those present as instructor to whom, as well as to the officiating priests, he shows his ability in medical magic, etc. He also seeks further information on the preparation of certain secret remedies and for this chooses a preceptor who has the reputation of possessing it. For acting as instructor, a Mide priest receives blankets, horses, and whatever may be mutually agreed upon between himself and his pupil.

The meetings take place at the instructor's wigiwam about two weeks apart, and at a time before he gets the degree, the candidate must go to a sudatory and take a vapor bath as a purgation, preparatory to his serious consideration of the sacred rites and teachings with which his mind "and heart" must thereafter be occupied, casting aside everything else from his thoughts. What the special peculiarities and ceremonials of initiation into the second degree may have been in olden times, it has been impossible to learn at this late day. The only special claims for benefits to be derived from the advancement in this as well as into the third and fourth degrees are that a Mide, on his admission into a new degree, receives the protection of that Manido alleged and believed to be the special guardian of such degree, and the repetition of the initiation adds to the magic powers previously received by the initiate. In the second degree the sacred migis is directed by the priests toward the joints of the body instead of the sides, head or heart.

THIRD DEGREE

The only difference in arrangement of the Mide-wigan in this, is the placing of a third degree post. The first post is set a short distance to the east of the middle of the floor, the second a little west of this, and the third about six or eight feet from the western door and is painted black, the others being the same as already described. The Makwa Manido- bear-spirit- is the tutelary guardian of this degree. The sudatory is the same size as for the second degree.

Usually one year passes before a Mide can be given the third degree even if he have the wherewithal to purchase it. Its price was three times that of the first degree and thus few presented themselves for it. The candidate chooses a Mide who at least has the third degree and gets his instruction as before, the same being a summing up of traditions and special medicine secrets, with tales of exploits in medication, incantation and exorcism.

A tradition of the Sun-spirit restoring life to a boy is an act exemplified by the Midewiwin ritual and a corruption of the original tradition is used in this degree. An outline of the same is given because of its value in this study of their ritual.

Once an old Mide with his wife and son started out on a hunting trip. The son died, and the mother went to the village to get the help of her father who was chief Mide priest, and whom she believed had the power to restore the boy to life. The chief Mide took three assistant Mide priests and went forth to the wigiwam where the body lay covered with robes.

The chief Mide placed himself at the left shoulder of the dead boy, the next in rank at the right, while the two assistants stationed themselves at the feet. Then the youngest Mide- he at the right foot of the deceased- began to chant a Mide song, which he repeated a second, a third and a fourth time. When he had finished, the Mide at the left foot sang a Mide song four times; then the Mide at the right shoulder did the same, after which the chief Mide priest sang his song four times, whereupon there was a perceptible movement under the blanket, and as the limbs began to move the blanket was taken off, when the boy sat up. Being unable to speak, he made signs that he wanted water which was given him. The Mide priests thereupon, each in turn as before, sang songs and gave the boy four pinches of powder which he was made to swallow. He then recovered his speech and told them that during the time his body had been in a trance, his spirit had been in the "spirit land" and had learned of the "grand medicine." He told his story thus:

He, the chief spirit of the Mide Society, gave us the "grand medicine," and he taught us how to use it. I have come back from the spirit land. There will be twelve, all of whom will take wives; when the last of these is no longer without a wife, then will I die. That is the time. The Mide spirit taught us to do right. He gave us life and told us how to prolong it. These things he taught us, and gave us roots for medicine. I give to you medicine; if your head is sick, this medicine put upon it, you will put it on.

This revelation to the boy was said to have been imparted to the Indians in the way recited. The number twelve referred to means three times the sacred number four, and that twelve priests shall succeed each other before death will come to the narrator. It will also be noticed that some of the words are archaic, which makes it appear that the tradition at least is ancient.

The preparations for the third degree are on the same order as for the others. After this, the candidate with the procession reaches the entrance of the Mide-wigan, when he and his instructor halt and the others go in and take their stations just within the door, facing the west. The drummers, who are seated in the southwestern angle of the enclosure, begin to drum and sing, while the candidate is led slowly around the outside, going by the south, thus following the course of the sun. Upon the completion of the fourth circuit he is halted directly opposite the main entrance, to which his attention is directed. The drumming and singing cease, the candidate beholds two Mide near the outer entrance on either side. These represent two evil Manidos, and guard the door against the entrance of those not duly prepared. The one on the northern side says to his companion, "Do you not see how he is formed?" The other answers, "Take care of it, the door."

The first then says, "Do you not see how he carries the goods?" The second replies in assent, and the instructor presents several pieces of tobacco to the two guards, when they allow him to enter as far as the inner entrance, where he is again stopped by two other guardian Manidos, who turn upon him as if to ask why he intrudes. The candidate holds out two parcels of tobacco and says, "Take it, the tobacco," which they do and stand aside, saying, "Go down," that is, "Follow the path." As the candidate is taken a few steps forward and toward the sacred stone, four of the eight officiating priests receive him; one who replaces the instructor, goes to the extreme western end and is joined by another, and they stand facing the east, while the other two stand side by side so as to face the west. It is believed that there are five powerful Manidos who abide in the third degree Mide-wigan, one of whom is the Mide-Manido- Kitshi Manido- one being present at the sacred stone and the first part where the gifts are deposited, the remaining three at the three degree posts.

As the candidate starts, and during his walk around the interior of the enclosure, the musicians sing and drum, while all those remaining are led to the left. As the candidate comes opposite the sacred stone he faces it and is turned around so that his back is not toward it in passing; the same is done at the second place where one of the spirits is supposed to abide, again at the first, second and third posts. By this time the candidate is at the western extremity of the structure, and as the second Mide receives him in charge, the other taking his station beside the preceptor, he continues his course toward the north and east to the point of departure, going through the same movements as before, in passing the three posts, the place of gifts and the sacred stone. This is done as an act of reverence to the Manidos and to acknowledge his gratitude for their presence and encouragement. When he again arrives at the eastern extremity of the enclosure he is placed between the two officiating Mide, who have been awaiting his return, while his companion goes farther back, even to the door, from which point he addresses the other officiating

Mide as follows: "Now is the time, I am telling (or advising), now is the time to be observed; I am ready to make him sit down."

Then one of the Mide priests standing beside the candidate leads him to the spot between the sacred stone and the first degree post where the blankets and other goods have been deposited, and here he is seated. This priest then walks slowly around him singing in a tremulous manner, "Wa, he, he, he, he, he, he," returning to a position so as to face him, when he says, freely translated:

"The time has arrived for you to ask of the Great Spirit this reverence (i. e., the sanctity of this degree). I am interceding in your behalf, but you think my powers are feeble; I am asking him to confer upon you the sacred powers. He may cause many to die, but I shall henceforth watch your course of success in life, and learn if he will heed your prayers and recognize your magic power."

When he has finished, the three others with their chief all seat themselves before the candidate. A Mide drum is given the chief Mide, and after drumming a short time, he becomes more and more inspired and sings a Mide song for such a time as he thinks his inspired condition calls for.

Then the officiating priests arise and the lowest one in rank grasps his Mide-sack and goes through the same acts of shooting the sacred migis into the joints and forehead of the candidate as before described. At the attempt made by the chief Mide, the candidate falls forward apparently unconscious. The priests then touch his joints and forehead with the upper end of their Mide-sacks, whereupon he recovers and rises to a standing position. The chief then addresses him thus: "You heed to what I say to you; if you are listening and will do what is right you will live to have white hair. That is all; you will do away with all bad actions."

INDIAN MASONRY

The second priest then says, "Never begrudge your goods, neither your tobacco nor your provisions." To which the candidate answers "Yes," meaning he will never regret what he has given the Mide for their services. He remains standing while the others take seats, when he goes to the pile of blankets, skins, etc., and after selecting appropriate gifts for the officiating priests, which he carries to them, he makes presents of less value to the other Mide present. Tobacco is distributed and while all are preparing to make an offering to Kitshi Manido, the candidate goes around to each member present and passing his hands down the sides of his head thanks him. The new member then finds a seat, and certain Mide appointed for the purpose bring in vessels of food which are carried around to the people present four distinct times. The feast continues for some time, after which the kettles and dishes are carried outside and all who wish indulge in smoking and Mide songs are chanted by the priests.

At the conclusion of the long ceremony, a few speeches are made recounting their powers and knowledge, when the chief priest calls upon them to adjourn and they all leave the Mide-wigan by the west door, and before night all the movable belonging are taken away. The evening is spent in visiting friends, dancing, etc., and on the next day they return to their homes.

FOURTH DEGREE

In this degree the Mide-wigan differs from the Others in having open doorways in both the northern and southern walls about the middle thereof and opposite each other. There are also four posts which stand at intervals between the place reserved for the gifts, and the western door. The sacred stone is a short distance from the eastern door. The first post is red with a band of green around the top, the second red with spots of white clay, to symbolize the sacred migis shell, and has perched upon it the stuffed skin of an owl- ko-ko-ko-o. The third post is black, but is square instead of round. The fourth post is nearest the western door and is in the shape of a cross, painted white, with red spots, except the lower half of the trunk which is squared, the colors upon the four sides being white on the east, green on the south, red on the west and black on the north.

About ten paces east of the main entrance, in a direct line between it and the sweat lodge, is planted a piece of thin board three feet high and six inches broad, the top of which is cut so as to present a three-lobed apex. The eastern side of this board is painted green, that facing the Mide-wigan red. Near the top is a small opening, through which the Mide are enabled to peep into the interior of the sacred structure to observe the angry Manidos occupying it and opposing the intrusion of anyone not of the fourth degree. A cedar tree is planted at each of the outer comers of the Mide-wigan, and about six paces from the north, west and south entrances a small brush structure is erected large enough to admit the body. These are termed bears' nests, supposed to be points where the bear Manido rested during the struggle passed through, while fighting with the evil Manidos within, to gain entrance and receive the fourth degree. Just within, and to either side of the east and west entrances, is planted a short post five feet high and eight inches thick, painted red on the side facing the interior and black on the reverse, at the base of each being laid a stone about the size of a human head. These four posts represent the four limbs and feet of the Bear Manido who made the four entrances and forcibly entered and expelled the evil beings who had opposed him. The fourth-degree post- the cross- symbolizes the four days' struggle at the four openings or doors in the north, south, east, and west walls of the structure.

Under ordinary circumstances it requires at least a year before a Mide of the third grade can proceed even though he be ready. The principal reason among most of the candidates is their inability to secure the fee, which is four times that of the first degree, and this will take him several years, and thus, it appears, few arrive at the distinction of the highest degree. When a candidate is ready, he makes it known to the chief and assistant Mide priests of the fourth degree, who hold a meeting in a wigiwam of one of their number to discuss the merits of the amount of his fee offered by him, and if the presents are numerous and valuable enough, his advancement is generally had without delay. When accepted; it is necessary for him to obtain the services of a renowned Mide, in order to acquire new or specially celebrated remedies or charms. The candidate may also give evidence of his own proficiency in magic without revealing the secrets of his success or the course he pursued to obtain it. The greater the mystery the higher he is held in esteem even by his jealous brethren.

There is not much to be gained by the preparatory instruction of the fourth degree, the chief claims being a renewal of the ceremony of "shooting the migis" into the body of the candidate, and enacting or dramatizing the traditional efforts of the Bear Mahido in his endeavor to receive from the Otter the secrets of this grade. One who succeeds becomes powerful in his profession and therefore more feared by the credulous. His sources of income are accordingly increased by the greater number of Indians who receive his assistance. The instructor, after settlement of the fees, receives the candidate and instructs him in the merits of magic compounds, making of charms, love powders, etc.

The candidate must take a sweat bath once each day for four successive days at some time during the autumn months of the year preceding his initiation. This is considered agreeable to Kitshi Manido, whose favor is constantly invoked that the candidate may be favored with the powers supposed to be conferred in the last degree.

As spring approaches the candidate makes occasional presents of tobacco to the chief priest and his assistants, and when the time for the annual ceremony approaches, they send out runners to members to ask their presence, and if of the fourth degree, their assistance.

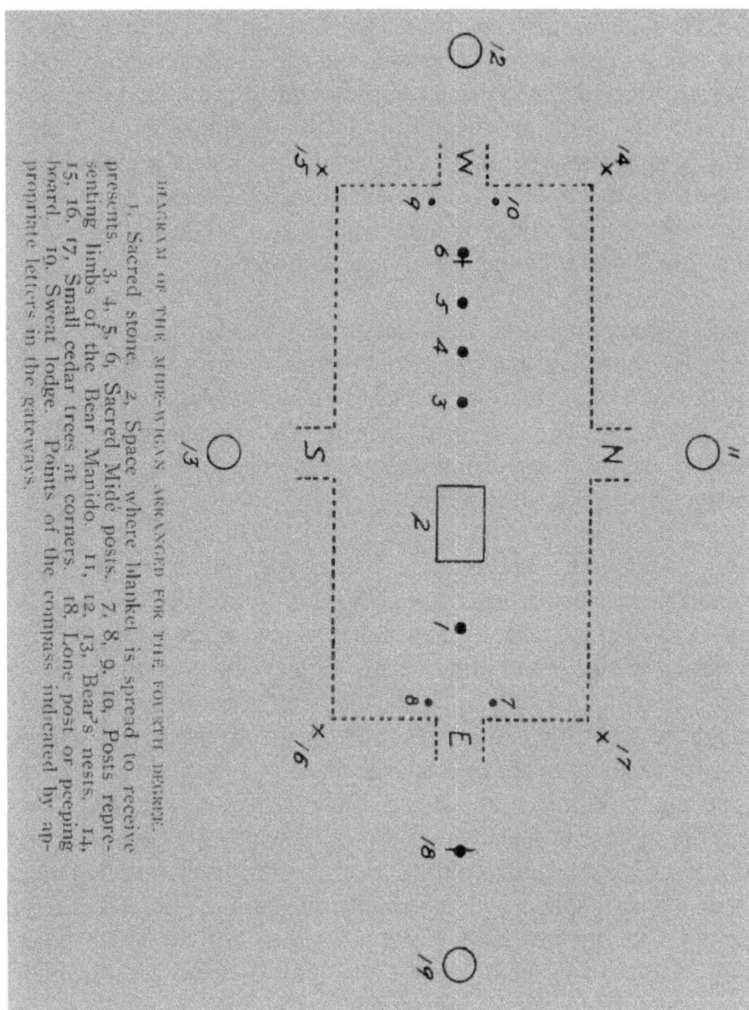

The candidate moves to the vicinity of the Mide-wigan so as to be able to go through the ceremony of purgation four times before the day of initiation. The sudatory is entered on the fifth day before the initiation, and after taking a sweat bath, he is joined by the preceptor, when both proceed to the four entrances of the Mide-wigan and deposit at each a small offering of tobacco. The same is done on the second and third days, but on the fourth the presents are also carried along and laid at the entrances, where they are received by assistants and suspended from the rafters of the interior. On the evening of the last day, the chief and officiating priests visit the candidate and his preceptor in the sweat lodge, have a ceremonial smoke and sing Mide songs. After this they talk over the initiation to take place the next day and having done this thoroughly they go to their wigiwams.

Early on the day of initiation the candidate goes to the sudatory and awaits his instructor. The priests arrive thereafter and are given tobacco, when all present join in a smoke offering to Kitshi Manido. The candidate takes his Mide drum and sings a song of hia own composition or one he may have bought of his instructor or some Mide priest.

After these preliminaries a procession is formed, the candidate and instructor gather up parcels of tobacco for gifts and take a place at the head of the column which moves toward the eastern entrance of the Mide-wigan. As they approach the lone post or board, the candidate halts, the priests continuing to chant and drum. The chief Mide goes to the board and peeps through the hole near the top to see the bad Manidos in the inside who are opposing the entrance of a stranger. This spot is supposed to represent the resting place or "nest" from which the Bear Manido looked on the evil spirits during the time of his imitation by the Otter. The evil spirits within are crouching on the floor, one behind the other, facing the east, the first being Mi-shi-bi-shi- the panther; the second, Me-shi-ke- the turtle; the third, Kwin'go-a'gi- the big wolverine; the fourth, Wa'-gush- the fox; the fifth, Ma-in'-gun- the wolf; and the sixth, Ma-kwa- the bear. They are the ones who endeavor to counteract or destroy the good wrought by the rites of the Midewiwin, and only by the aid of the good Manidos can they be driven from the Mide-wigan so as to allow a candidate to enter and receive the benefits of the degree. The second Mide then looks upon the group of evil beings, then the third and lastly the fourth priest. They then advise the presentation of tobacco at that point to invoke the best efforts of the Mide Manidos in his behalf.

It is asserted that all of the evil Manidos who occupied and surrounded the preceding degree structures have now assembled about this fourth degree Mide-wigan to make a final effort against the admission and advancement of the candidate; so he impersonates the good Bear Manido, and is obliged to follow a similar course in going from his present position to the door of the structure. Upon hands and knees he slowly crawls toward the main entrance, when a wailing voice is heard in the east, which sounds like the word "Ha-n" prolonged in a monotone. This is Ge-gi-si-bi-ga-ne-dat' Manido. His bones are heard rattling as he approaches; he wields his bow and arrow; his long hair streaming in the air, and his body covered with migis shells from the salt sea from which he has just come to help in driving out the opposing spirit. This being the information given the candidate, he assumes and personates the character of the Manido referred to, and being given a bow and four arrows, and under the guidance of his instructor, he proceeds toward the main entrance while the officiating priests enter and station themselves within the door facing west. The preceptor carries the remaining parcels of tobacco, and on reaching the door the candidate makes four movements with his bow and arrow toward the interior, as if shooting, the last time sending an arrow within, upon which the grinning spirits are forced to retire toward the other end of the enclosure. The candidate then rushes in at the main entrance, and on coming out at the south suddenly turns and again employs his bow and arrow four times toward the crowd of evil Manidos, who have rushed toward him while he was within. At the last gesture of shooting into the enclosure, he sends forward an arrow, lays down a parcel of tobacco and crouches to rest at the so-called "bear's nest." The Mide priests continue to drum and sing, while he rests. Then the candidate approaches the southern door again, on all fours, and the moment he arrives there, he rises and is hurried through the enclosure to emerge in the west where he turns again suddenly and makes the same movements of shooting arrows, then gets down in the western "bear's nest." After a short interval he approaches this door on hands and knees and goes through the same process, coming out at the northern door, where at the fourth menace he sends an arrow among the spirits. These are now greatly disturbed by the magic power of the candidate, and the assistance given him by the Mide Manidos, so that they are obliged to seek safety in flight. After resting in the "bear's nest" opposite the northern door, he goes in through it in the same manner and is hurried toward the eastern door, where he turns around and seeing but a few angry Manidos left, he takes his last arrow and aiming it at them makes four threatening gestures toward them and sends the arrow into the structure, which puts to flight all opposition on the part of this host of Manidos. The path now being clear, he deposits another gift of tobacco at the door and is led within, the instructor receives his bow and lays the remaining tobacco on the pile of blankets and robes that have now been removed from the rafters and laid on the ground midway between the sacred Mide stone and the first Mide post.

The chief Mide priest now takes charge of the candidate and says: "Now is the time (to take) the path that has no end. Now is the time I shall inform you (of) that which I was told, the reason I live." The second priest says, "The reason I now advise you is that you may heed him when he speaks to you." The candidate is then led around the interior of the enclosure, the assistant Mide fall in line of march followed by all others present except the musicians. During the circuit, which is performed slowly, the chief Mide drums on the Mide drum and chants. By the time the chant is completed the head of the procession is where it started just within the eastern door, the members return to their seats, only the four officiating Mide remaining with the candidate and instructor. To search further that no evil Manidos remain lurking within the Mide-wigan, the chief priests lead the candidate in a zigzag manner to the western door and back again to the east. In this way the path leads past the side of the Mide stone, then right oblique to the north of the heap of presents, thence left oblique to the south of the first degree post, then passing the second on the north and so on until the last post is reached, around which the course continues, and back in a similar serpentine manner to the eastern door.

The candidate is then led to the pile of blankets and seated, the four officiating priests placing themselves before him, the instructor standing back near the first of the four degree posts.

The candidate then kneels, the fourth Mide goes to him and shoots the sacred migis into his breast as before described, followed in the same way by the third, second and first priests, the last one alone shooting his migis into the candidate's forehead, on which he falls forward, spits out a migis shell which he had previously secreted in his mouth, and upon the priests rubbing upon his back and limbs their Mide sacks he recovers and resumes his sitting posture.

The officiating priests then go to either side of the enclosure, when the newly initiated member rises and with the help of his instructor distributes the gifts and thanks those present as in the other degrees, and the gathering together and feast, follow as on other occasions.

The Midewiwin Society had a system of facial decoration for each of their four degrees. For example the first degree colors were a broad green band across the forehead and a narrow strip of vermilion across the face, just below the eyes.

VIII

ESOTERIC SOCIETIES OF THE ZUNI

After the remainder of this work had all been written, it was thought best to place in it the present chapter, notwithstanding a desire to confine ourselves to the nomadic tribes. There is no doubt that much of great interest to Masons will be found among the southwestern and Mexican Indians, but that is a subject which the writer hopes the future will give him time and means to investigate on the ground.

These Zuni societies, while embracing religious tenets and ceremonies, such as invocations for rain, crops, success in the hunt, etc., also have for their object the healing of the sick. They are to a large degree medicine societies, but by no means confined to that, it should be understood.

To entitle one to membership in the A'pitlashi-wanni, one must not only have killed an enemy, but have brought in the scalp- at least such was the custom until more recent years. The stopping of war among the tribes, with the following shortage of scalps, has lessened the numbers of this society, in many things the most powerful in Zuni, so that men who have never fought the enemy are received into the fraternity, and the ceremony of initiation occurs exactly as if they were genuine victors, an old scalp from the scalp house, without a vestige of hair, being used in place of a fresh scalp.

When the fraternities meet for initiation, they convene during four days- for three nights until midnight and on the fourth until sunrise. The Little Fire and Cimex fraternities meet in March, once in four years. The Newekwe (Galaxy fraternity), embraces the orders of Onayanakia and Itsepcho and has a Kok-ko-thlanna, or Great God, as a patron god. The practices of this order in obeying the supposed commands of the god, as for example, the use of excrement with their "medicine," so it will not burn the intestines, are so revolting that we feel impelled to omit details, which might be made plainer in private conversation, for the purpose of studying the vague peculiarities of the human race in its primitive condition, just as we would examine the condition of modem fanatics among us.

Parts of the ceremonies of the Newekwe are, how- ever, interesting and agreeable, with these vile parts thrust aside. In the ceremonial chamber of the fraternity just spoken of is arranged an elaborately decorated altar at the west end of a long room. Above the altar, extending across the room, is a bar, representing the galaxy, on which stand two figures of Payatamu, a god. The central part of the bar is composed of cloud symbols with seven stars representing Ursa Major. The sun's face is shown by a disk of blue-green, surrounded by blocks of black and white, which denote the house of the clouds. Carved birds, suspended from the blue-green, serrated clouds of the bar, represent Ehotsi, the bat. Birds perched on the clouds of the upper portion of the bar, represent the bird of the zenith. Lightning is symbolized by zigzag carvings at each end of the bar upon which the figures of Payatamu stand. The pendent eagle plumes symbolize the breath of life, which is Awona-wilona, the supreme power. The tablet altar is composed of cloud symbols, the sun surrounded by the house of the clouds, the morning and evening stars carved on the tops of the rear posts and painted in white each side of the sun. The yellow lion of the north, and blue-green of the west are represented on the front posts, each of which has two hawk plumes standing from the top. A dark stone animal about two feet high is sitting before the altar. The flute of the fraternity, a medicine bowl and a prayer meal basket are placed before the altar. The star of the four winds, each point decorated with a star and cumulus clouds (the serrated ends), from which hang eagle cast plumes, is suspended above the altar. A large stone animal fetish stands before the altar on the north and has a lynx skin over it at times.

The stone animal is said to be their great grandfather of mystery medicine, and was converted into stone at the time when the great fire spread over the earth.

After a meal the men form in groups and prepare plume offerings, which are spears of grass combined with feathers or plumes. For the initiation a parallelogram is outlined in white meal on the floor. This is afterwards filled in with meal. A line of black encloses the whole, and segments of circles, symbolic of rain clouds, are formed in black upon the white ground. A black line is run transversely across the parallelogram. Two figures are also delineated in black on the ground color, one representing Bitsitsi, who is the jester and musician god, the other his younger brother, and horizontal black lines cross the figures from top of the head to feet.

After completion of the prayer plumes, each man lights a reed, filled with native tobacco, and, drawing a mouthful of smoke, puffs it through the feathers. The smoking of the cigarette is repeated three times, and the prayer plumes are then gathered by one of the fraternity and deposited in a basket tray which is placed by the altar. Later the members of the choir group themselves in the southwest end of the room, the women sitting on the north side. The large animal fetish is behind the altar at this time. The flutist also stands behind the altar. The medicine man who sits on the north side of the altar then proceeds to prepare the medicine water. This water is consecrated, and after that the medicine man takes a plume offering separately from the basket, and sprinkles the water. He then dips the water with a shell and, takings it into his mouth, throws a spray over the plumes. After the offerings are all sprinkled, the director wraps them in corn husks in groups of twos and fours and returns them to the basket tray.

During the pauses in the long ritual, jokes are indulged in and the Catholic priest is mimicked. The weird performance continues all night, when the god appears to administer his medicine, and here we draw the line.

Another Zuni fraternity, the Saniakiakwe, also called Suskikwe (Coyote), has two orders- Hunters and Fire. The members of the latter order do not eat fire, but they play with large, live coals and rub them over their bodies. It is not deemed best to give details of the ceremonies of all the fraternities of the Zuni as it would take space beyond the scope of this volume, and an example has already been presented. The account of the grand medicine lodge of the Ojibwa will also supply a wealth of detail which will make clear the object of this work.

In the Zuni ceremonies we find in some form the same things elsewhere dealt with. In those of the Arrow fraternity the company initiating a candidate encircle some decorated, sacred boxes in the plaza four times, when all stand for a moment shouting "Ha-ha-ha." The arrow director then steps before the boxes, facing them, waves his arrow from right to left over them, then, waving it in a circle, turns from right to left and goes through the form of swallowing his arrow, facing east. Others then do this swallowing performance, groups of two facing the cardinal points while doing so.

In the initiation into the order of Onayanakia, the director forms a cross of meal, symbolic of the four regions, upon the stone floor near the altar, and places the medicine bowl in the center, and his prey god fetishes at the points of the cross, and those for the zenith and nadir by the side of the one at the eastern tip. Ashes are thrown first to the east, then to the north, west, south, zenith and nadir, for the physical purification of those present. Live coals are held in the mouth as long a time as one minute, and a good natured rivalry exists as to who can hold a fiery coal the longest. In their marches they pass around the altar from the south side.

The Shumaakwe is a fraternity named from Shuminne, a spiral shell, because this fraternity treats the disease known as

Kusukiayakia, which is a terrible twisting of the body- that is, convulsions. During the initiation ceremonies, there is a dance wherein a circle of about twenty dancers is formed. They dance around from left to right, symbolic of the road or pathway of life. Two young men who personate Saiapa gods are in the center of the circle. The two young men dance back and forth in the circle, which is constantly moving, with a monotonous side-step. This dance continues about thirty minutes, when all the dancers pass to the altar and inhale the sacred breath of life. Shumaikoli, or gods, represented by members, appear successively in regular order and join the dances. After the god of the north comes the one of the west with blue face mask, then red for the south, white for the east, all color for the zenith, and black for the nadir. The cloud decorations on the face masks differ.

IX

COMPARISONS

Let us now recall some of those things which, in reading about the ceremonies of the Mide-wiwin, forced themselves upon us as being common to the Indian and white man, even though the forms were not alike in minute detail. However much we might wish, and seek to place our beloved Masonry on a pedestal all by itself, and cast down the idols of Lo, the poor Indian, they will not down, but rise before us in shadowy protest, quite in the same way as do those wondrous things arranged for us by our old priests, and to which we render homage under the sacred name of "Landmarks of Masonry."

We found indisputable statements that in their ritual peculiar words and idioms known only to their ancient language were used and were seldom if ever heard in ordinary conversation. The Mason will recall many such words and sentences in our own rituals, which he found it necessary to have repeated to him, and then demanded the meaning thereof. This use of ancient forms and words naturally betokens the establishment of the ritual in the time when those obsolete words were in use and helps us date back. Thus we easily trace our own laws to the old common law Of England, by means of many a quaint phrase or word, of by a Norman, French or Latin term.

The Cherokee myths deal with the west and the spirit land in most beautiful terms. They call it Usunhi-yi, which is the twilight land- "where it is always growing dark"- the spirit land in the west. This is the word used in the sacred formulas instead of the ordinary word Wude-lingun-yi, "where it sets." In the same way Nunda'-yi or Nundagun-yi, the "sun place, or region," is the formulistic name for the east instead of Digalungun-yi, "where it (the sun) comes up," the ordinary term. These archaic expressions give to myths and formulas a peculiar beauty which is lost in translation. The interpreter once said, "I love to hear these old words." And thus it is that the Mason loves to hear "cowans" instead of "intruders" in his ritual and refuses to change.

It seems that much information was lost by the Indians through the deaths of their aged predecessors, who neglected to deposit their secrets in a safe and secure place where they might be found by future generations should they become lost. All the teachings of the mystics is that a knowledge of what is beyond was once possessed by man but has been lost. In the Great Light we read that Enoch walked with God; that is no more than that he had that which is lost; he knew the Logos, the word. That is what the statement means just the same as that H. A. had the word. It is not at all absurd to venture the assertion that there was a time when men knew these things; that they knew exactly what was over on the other shore and knew their immortal souls clearer than we do now. There were certain arts like the making of malleable glass, Tyrian purple and Damascus steel, which men once knew but are now known as the lost arts, and marvelous they once were. Man has forgotten or lost some wonderful things. That is looking backward.

INDIAN MASONRY

Could the people of ancient times have looked forward, they would have seen in the great distance, steam engines, dynamos and other appliances to seize, control and use the giant forces which surround us on every hand. Yet the water of running streams, the steel and copper and material of every kind existed in exactly the same conditions and forms thousands of years ago buried in the rubbish of the temple of the whole earth. They had these things in the same great abundance as we have and if they had possessed the knowledge could have made the same use of them. Who knows but there may have been a great civilization which did this and far more, but which has been lost with all its wonders? For, if man has lost and forgotten, he learns and progresses, so he may yet more get the true word. Does there not come a sober serious moment, some time in the midst of earth's know the beyond while here in earthly life and once cares and joys when the Mason has, or should take thought on these things? Was there not some one time, brother, when you really had an intense and earnest longing to know whether you will indeed be raised and received among the brethren in an eternal lodge? When you shall indeed know the great secret you have labored for- aye more than seven years? Newton discovered a force called gravity, but he never discovered its cause. The intensity of its force diminishes with the increase of distance between the bodies, inversely as the squares of the distance at which it is exerted. Gravity can neither be produced nor destroyed! It acts equally between all pairs of bodies, the acceleration of each body being proportional to the mass of the other. It is neither hindered nor strengthened by any intervening medium; it occupies no time in its transmission; its force is governed by an unfailing, regular rule. The Spiritualists claim that by spiritual means they can render buoyant bodies heavier than air, and this they call levitation. We smile because it is like the dreams of the alchemists. Yet modem science is demonstrating that the so-called "elements" are not simple substances, but there is a finite atom yet to be determined, from which all combinations are made. As one writer aptly puts it when asked to prove the transmutation of metals, "I may be able to demonstrate to your entire satisfaction that there is a mountain of gold in the moon, and yet not be able to place one ounce in your hand, and so it is with the atoms and the elements."

Since Newton's time, no one ever found out the cause of that mysterious, all pervading power of gravity, the energy governed with such clock-like regularity. This does not establish that this mighty secret may not at some time be learned by someone and made known to his brethren. In possession of a knowledge of the cause, the way to control it may be also learned and the Spiritualist's dream may be realized! In a like way the great secret of the beyond may be unlocked at some future period and again be made known to man, and he be enabled to see that beyond while yet in the flesh.

In the third degree the Indian candidate is halted before the main entrance, to which his attention is directed. This entrance is in the east and we halt our F. C. there and direct his attention to the same place.

Their candidate, having been prompted, says, "Let me come in and put down my gifts," i. e., he must signify that it is of his own free will he seeks admission. He is also, as with us, instructed that his thoughts must dwell on the seriousness of the course he is pursuing and the sacred character of his new life. He receives the "grand medicine," and is told to always take care of it, that is, the secrets of the degree.

The Redman sends out invitation twigs or sticks for the lodge ceremonies, and they require attendance or a good excuse. These have all the requisites of a summons. He has birch bark charts. These are by no means symbolic, but they aid him in carrying out his ritual, and for the same purpose of helping the memory, they correspond to our own charts. It is, however, understood that ours go farther and contain symbols. When the Mide candidate is initiated, he has presented to him a new Mide-sack which is worn upon his person, while we present our candidate an apron for the same purpose. A time must elapse between his degrees, and he must select an instructor who is learned in the Midewiwin, and who instructs him before he can take another degree, and this is what we also do.

The Ojibwas have a tradition of the death of a boy, and a procession of priests who went to raise him from the dead, and in doing so they took particular stations about the body. On being brought to life the boy describes twelve priests which will succeed each other.

Here we have the number twelve and this may be compared to the twelve F. C. so that the tradition may be easily recognized by the Mason.

Now this tradition is likewise carried out in substance in their ceremonies. There is the march about the Mide lodge four times by the south in the course of the sun. It will be noted that the members stop in their proper places and the officiating priests have stations to which they go. It stands out clearly that the candidate takes the part of one who is killed and brought to life. The Chief Priest, after the candidate has fallen in semblance of death, raises the sacred migis in the east, south, west, north, and to the sky. This may be likened to the recognition of a certain jewel formerly worn by an illustrious personage. Then the procession is formed and marches about the body. The priests make an effort to raise it but do not succeed; whereupon the Chief Mide Priest touches the body with his Mide-sack, saying, "Arise," and it is brought to life.

It needs but a little analysis, without much stretch of the imagination, to discern striking features in the Zuni ceremonies which will commend themselves to the observant Mason. The pendent eagle plumes above the altar stand in the place of the letter G, which ought properly to be the triangle, and they all mean the same. Then there is the star of the four winds which may be likened to the blazing star. It no doubt has its origin as far back as Anubis of the Egyptians. The explanations given in monitors are about as satisfactory for the blazing star as the stories of Santa Claus, accepted in childhood, are to the adult.

Again we note that the Zunis formerly were genuine scalp takers and none but a victor in war could be initiated. Now the Zuni is given his degree with an old scalp and never takes one. This is exactly the transition from operative Masonry to speculative. The working tools of Masons are no longer actual but symbolical only. Men are received who not only never did a stroke of operative craft work but know absolutely nothing about even the rudiments thereof. They could not tell a frieze, entablature, architrave or shaft from a hole in the wall. In the dance of the Shu-maakwe there is a distinct approach to the point within the circle.

There are noticeable evidences that the Indians maintained the phallic religion. Looking once again to the dim past we find that two pillars stood before the entrance of Phoenician temples, as Greek authors often mention, and Phoenician seafarers explained the rocks on either side of the Straits of Gibraltar as the "Pillars of Melkart," or as the Greeks translated it, "Pillars of Hercules," a name which they retained until Spain was conquered by the Moors, who called the northern rock after their leader Gebel el Tarik, the rock of Tarik, since abbreviated into Gibraltar. These rocks stood at the boundaries of the known world, the same as the pillars before the temples, and were adopted as the same emblems. Before the Jewish Temple stood the two columns Jachin and Boaz as they do now before the Masonic temple. It may seem downright harsh to set aside the common Masonic explanations and put these pillars back in the old junk pile of pagan symbols, but truth will out, for they were indeed phallic symbols. We need not be surprised, therefore, to find "degree posts" in the lodge of the Midewiwin. Stone worship was common among some tribes of the American Indians, and we know that in spite of the crudity of their views, their sentiments are marked by a deep-seated religious awe. The Roman Catholic sets up roadside monuments and it is but a return to the custom of Jacob who set up a Matsebah or stone, and the ancient Egyptian obelisk. That the Catholics set up the identical thing is not claimed, but they do set up statuettes of the virgin, saints or emblem of the cross, and behind it is the same old, very old idea.

I have examined a number of the rough stone pestles and mortars which were unquestionably made and used by the Indians. These are in the possession of the Oregon Historical Society and one mortar and pestle found in 1899 were taken out 27 feet underground in a railroad grade, so the curator, Mr. Geo. H. Himes, told me. He also showed me a pestle taken from beneath a large fir stump, which had been blasted out on the Grande Ronde Indian Reservation in eastern Oregon. He said he counted more than three hundred rings on the stump, which indicates the great age of the pestle which had lain beneath it undisturbed. Some of these pestles are so plainly formed and marked that the significance of all of them in connection with mortars as phallic symbols is beyond question. Those who try to trace the psychology of this discover, at the bottom of such a primeval form of worship, the groping after a purer and more spiritual faith, for which the untrained mind of the savage did not find itself able to give abundant expression.

There is also a striking feature in the attempts of the candidate to enter at the four gates of the lodge and his repulse by the bad, opposing spirits. Also in his creeping toward these entrances, which may remind us of the movements under a living arch. These scenes are easily to be recognized, so that comparisons may be made, and more comment on them is unnecessary. Again, in his sermon or charge, the Mide chief speaks of being raised from the dead and the language is not at all far apart from that supposed to have been uttered by K. S.

No doubt the reader will also have noticed a remarkable

feature of the Mide council in its sacred stone, which is used in all the degrees, and it appears the candidate must not have his back to it. It is therefore an object which demands a certain reverence and bearing toward it as distinctive as in the case of the Masonic altar. In fact it was his altar.

The Indian Mide, including the candidates, put on their best clothing to attend lodge. They likewise partook of a repast at the close of lodge, had their speeches during this time and left their lodge for home by way of the west door.

It is also noticeable that there is a repetition of songs, words and acts. This is common to Masonic rituals and is an underlying feature of religious worship generally. The pious Catholic tells his beads in prayer daily. Rituals of the Catholic and Episcopal churches, which are among the oldest, have constant repetition of words and phrases.

In the matter of banquets, there is absolutely no difference between the Indian and the Mason, and in this respect each is alike in his lodge- he will eat, talk and smoke there. In other things there is only a difference in the details, as I have pointed out, but not in the final meaning and objects.

X

PIN INDIANS

This work will not be complete without a short account of what our Indian of today does in the way of a lodge on "improved lines."

When the Indian of modem times, long under the influence of the white race, sought to form a new society, it was very natural that the ideas, forms and ceremonies of the Anglo-Saxon should be clearly stamped upon the product. It is no more possible for the Redman now to make a ritual and ceremony purely Indian, after the all powerful lordship of the stronger race, than it is possible for the white man, with all his cunning and skill, to make a ritual and ceremony which would be an imitation of the old Midewiwin so close as to deceive. It only goes to show that those things which have passed away shall be no more, and that the prouder race should not exult in its power but read seriously what is writ by the hand of time. It will be of much interest, I am sure, to bring back to those who lived in war times the memory of the "Pin Indians," and to those Masons who never heard of them, the account in this work will be another item for their store of knowledge.

There was a certain Cherokee secret society which obtained some newspaper notice years ago. It had for its principal object the promotion of Cherokee autonomy. Its name was properly Kituhwa but was commonly spelled Ketoowah in English print. The Indian name was derived from the ancient town of the old Cherokee Nation and the society embraced the most conservative men of the tribe and it sometimes stood for the name of the nation itself as it was originally, Ani-kituhwagi (people of Kituhwa).

A strong bond of comradeship, if not a regular social organization, appears to have existed among the warriors and leading men of the various settlements of the Kituhwa districts from a remote period, so that the name is even now used in councils as indicative of genuine Cherokee feeling in its highest patriotic form. Some years ago when delegates from the western nation visited brethren beyond the Mississippi, the speaker for the delegates expressed their fraternal feeling for their separated kinsmen by saying in his opening speech, "We are all Kituhwa people (Ani-kituhwagi)."

The modern Ketoowah Society in the Cherokee Nation was organized shortly before the Civil war by John B. Jones, son of the missionary Evan Jones and an adopted citizen of the nation. Its ostensible purpose was to cultivate a national feeling among the full bloods, in opposition to the innovations of the mixed bloods. The real purpose, however, was to counteract the influence of the "Blue Lodge" and other secret secession organizations among the wealthier slave-holding classes, made up chiefly of mixed bloods and whites. It extended to the Creeks, and its members in both tribes rendered good service to the Union cause throughout the war. They were frequently known as "Pin Indians." Since the close of the war the society has distinguished itself by its determined opposition to every scheme looking to the curtailment or destruction of Cherokee national self-government. The facts about the society are about as follows: Those Cherokees who were loyal to the Union combined in a secret organization for self-protection, assuming the designation of Ketoowah Society, which name was soon merged into that of "Pins." The Pins were so styled because of a peculiar manner they adopted of wearing a pin. The symbol was discovered by their enemies, who applied the term in derision, but it was accepted by the loyal league and has almost superseded the designation which its members first assumed.

The Pin organization was begun among the members of the Baptist congregation at Peavine, Going-Snake District in Cherokee Nation. In a short time the society numbered nearly 3,000 men and had commenced proselyting Creeks when the Rebellion, against which it was arming, prevented its further extension, the poor Creeks having been driven into Kansas by the rebels of the Golden Circle Society. During the war the Pins rendered services to the Union cause in many bloody encounters, as has been acknowledged by our generals. It was distinctively an anti-slavery organization. The slave-holding Cherokees who constituted the wealthy and more intelligent class, naturally allied themselves with the South, while loyal Cherokees became more and more opposed to slavery. This was clearly shown when the legislature first met in 1863. They not only abolished slavery unconditionally and forever, before any slave state made a movement toward emancipation, but they made any attempt at enslaving a grave misdemeanor.

The secret signs of the Pins were a peculiar way of touching the hat as a salutation, particularly when they were too far apart for recognition in other ways. They had a peculiar mode of taking hold of the lapel of the coat, first drawing it away from the body. During the war a portion of them were forced into the Rebellion, but quickly rebelled against General Cooper, who was placed over them, and when they fought against the general at Bird Creek, they wore a bit of corn-husk, split into strips, tied in their hair. In the night when two Pins met and one asked the other, "Who are you?" the reply or pass was "Tahlequah. Who are you?" The response was, "I am Ketoowah's son."

Such is the interesting account of the attempts made by Indians of later times to form a secret society, as related by Dr. D. J. MacGowan and by members of the Ethnological Bureau.

XI

LESSONS

There is no Indian Masonry. There is Indian Masonry. This wide difference I make clear when I say, no Indian Masonry as the average man understands it, but there is a deep Indian Masonry for him who seeks to find it.

Many are accustomed to say that the only good Indian is the dead one. Suppose that, stung by injustice, or what he thought was such, he took to the war-path and wrought maddened vengeance upon the whites? The paleface mobs have pursued innocent men whom they believed guilty of some dark crime, and killed them. Something makes women hang around with bated breath to see the low Igorrotes kill and cook a miserable dog, as good a friend as man ever had, and better than some men by far.

How differs this from the savage? He has a little the best of it, because the white is a savage with a thin veneer of civilization which has not yet gone any too deeply into him, although he has had some centuries the start of the savage. He ought to know better- he does, but the savage in him breaks forth into a fierce flame, which burns off all the veneer in a second and he must then needs do penance until he gets a veneer of whitewash. All religions have some lowering things about them. All races have some low habits and have men of low brain power, and those whose thoughts are of the highest, born to lead others. The Redman, even in his simple way, with a fair chance, will display all the good qualities of faith, hope and charity, brotherly love and relief. There are, no doubt, among them those who know the inmost soul and the Grand Architect, far better than many a man of quick business brain, who swiftly hunts the almighty dollar upon shifting sands, in the teeming marts of this mind-straining country, but who has no time to take thought of nature, or nature's God, or the duty he owes to his fellow man. Shall we Masons, who tell the E. A. of the universality of Masonry, dare to say that the Indian is not a Mason?

An interesting institution was found among the Wyandottes and some other tribes- that of fellowship. Two young men agree to be friends forever, or more than brothers. Each tells the other the secrets of his life, advises with him on important matters and defends him from wrong and violence and at his death is his chief mourner. Here are, in full reality, all the elements of a Masonic lodge. Those men were Masons in their hearts.

There is no Indian Masonry in that small and narrow sense which most of us think of; that is, one who pays lodge dues, wears an apron like ours and gives signs so nearly like ours that we find him perforce a Mason in any degree or degrees we know, and which degrees we are too prone to watch, just as we do a procession of historical floats, which casually interest us, and maybe a little more so if we can but secure a place at the head of the procession, the true meaning of which we have but a faint idea about. This makes our own Masonry as meaningless as the interpretation of Indian signs by an ignorant trapper.

There is a wide and a distinct difference, it should be remembered, between the esoteric societies of the Egyptians and modern Masonic societies, notwithstanding the great pretensions of the latter to superior knowledge, occult philosophy and a "secret." The Egyptian priests were really scientists who discussed their science in secret. They conversed about a deep philosophy and all this was covered up beneath imposing ceremonies provided for an ignorant populace, which would no doubt have killed them had they not preserved and performed the old rituals coming down from time out of mind. Modem Masonry has no such motive to preserve science, for the world has come unto its own and is now liberal toward all science and men of science. The Mason, however, hangs fast to his "degrees," which he puts into the candidate much as the Ojibwa shot the sacred migis at his candidate. Those Indians could not give the natural history story of the otter who furnished the bag for the migis shell, neither did they know any scientific facts about shells. The Mide sack simply contained a few trifles and was a "great secret,"- wonderful medicine! The modem Mason is getting back, not to the position of the Egyptians, for that is no longer necessary, but to the position of the Indian- idle curiosity and zeal for a so-called secret.

We are all free to be Masons, but there are many accepted Masons who are not Masons and never will be. They do not ask anything greater or higher than to be lip-serving ritualists, to mumble words they do not understand, and to give signs or tokens to prove nothing more than that they were accepted at the door and it was opened in the hope that they might in time see Masonic light. So they walked in, having been, most secretly, first prepared in their hearts to be made Shriners, and expecting to break their necks, if necessary, to get over the road to that which seems to them to be the loftiest pinnacle of Masonry- the real thing! Alas, vain hope! It is most deeply to be regretted, but nevertheless true, for I have had the profane about to petition a lodge ask me, not how much they can learn of real Masonry, but "How soon can I get through?" No doubt many who read these lines have had this same experience. There is much of the ape in man. Yawn freely a few times as though naturally, and you can very easily cause several about you to do likewise and others will unconsciously have the desire to yawn, even though they check themselves. They do not know why they yawn; neither do many Masons know why they give signs and tokens; they do so like parrots. This is not Masonry. It is these very things which have encouraged the fierce criticism of those who oppose Masonry and who claim it is but an evil device to keep men from home and family. It is this which keeps Masonry from being seated as firmly as it should in the high and honorable place which belongs to it before all mankind.

There is more than money and material things to be gained in this life. Brethren, my voice is and shall be lifted up for a firm stand on the side of true Masonic principles. I will be heard until there are enough voices raised with mine to call, in one great tone of thunder, for the cleaning out of the temple of Masonry, even as Christ drove the mercenary ones out of the temple of long ago, that it might be used for those spiritual purposes it was intended for. Cry out, brethren- down with the shams and counterfeits passed upon us every day as genuine Masonry! Every man having a right to vote here as a citizen is protected by all the might and power of our great country, and he is called upon and agrees, when he has these rights, to give true and faithful allegiance to our country, which aims to place every man equal with his fellows. What say you then of the man who breaks a law, whether secretly or openly, and by so doing wrongs his fellows? Is he branded as a traitor? Are traitors only those who levy war by sheer open force of arms against the government? Are they not traitors, but benefactors, who have seized power; and for the sake of greater profits to themselves, will cheat, wrong, defraud, and oppress those who must labor so hard and so long that they have no time to study or think of their rights or a remedy to get them? Those who must even put their women and children to work in factories that they may live? Are men who slander, blackmail and do dirty tricks in business to get ahead of or ruin their competitors, good citizens, or traitors to the commonweal? Are newspaper writers, speakers, preachers and all who lead the people, honest citizens, when they spread false reports or give aid and comfort to those who do such things during times of peace, or are they secret enemies of the people? Are such an honor to Masonry? Our brother, the Redman, made every one run the gauntlet to prove himself worthy and well qualified. It is surely time, brethren, that Masonry should call upon its members to follow in letter and spirit the oath of allegiance which the applicant takes, when he agrees on his sacred honor that he will keep within the influence of a desire for knowledge and a sincere wish to be serviceable to his fellow men! Is Masonry becoming cowardly, that it fears those in high places, or who have a political pull? Must unworthy members be received, because someone forsooth says they will be an honor to Masonry?

No man who is not a good citizen, secretly and openly, has any right to go into Masonry, or to stand as a Mason among Masons, if he has succeeded in breaking in, no matter how supposedly high he is in society, business, politics or religion. Condemn not, however, without a most careful investigation. Hesitate not to act when action is necessary. The humblest brother who toils with his hands daily, and patiently bears his lot, yet has within him a true, kind and brotherly heart and genuine love for his country, is a peer among Masons and among men. When that brother goes to his last rest in the cheapest kind of a shroud and coffin, he is still nobler in the sight of God and all true Masons than is he whose money, position and so-called influence are put forth as his claims to great honors at the hands of Masonry, when he lacks the very jewels of the Fellowcraft. I want to meet and be often with that humble brother while traveling here on the level of time, and afterwards in the great beyond. He would shine here in the master's chair, and over there I know he will be found very near to the Grand Architect and in far closer unison with him than the other.

The Redman teaches us a mighty lesson, for in his simple life he did not seek great offices, great wealth and great material influence to overcome the whole country for the benefit of a handful of chiefs. He truly sought after the immortality of his soul and the Great Spirit. There is no taint of politics or mercenary motives in his lodge to tarnish the sincerity of his search for the beyond. He allowed no costly pews, or furnishings, no ceremonies, no holding of office in lodge or tribe to turn him aside from what he deemed the right path. He was sincere in the light he had.

He never mentioned the name of Kitshi Manido, the Great Spirit, except with reverence and an offering of tobacco. His preparation room was his sweat lodge and there he must invariably be purified in the most thorough manner of which the human system is capable. This time for purification might be shortened under special circumstances, but this did not happen by any means so often as a candidate now gets his "hurry up dispensation," and goes through in sweating time, just as though there were no lodges in the place he journeys to, which could and would give him his degrees in an orderly and painstaking way. The Indian masters were not so easy to work in this respect.

In the Mide charge given by their priests they told the candidate to do what is right, to enjoy life and do away with bad actions. They also taught charity. We surely have no greater principles in our own charges. In spite of some of his sleight-of-hand tricks, and what we would call foolish mummeries, the Indian did have a most profound veneration and respect for the Great One, wherever he is and Whoever he may be, as also for the future happiness of his own soul and the souls of all his tribe.

Our Bro. Roosevelt says in his masterly message of Dec.

5, 1905, teeming with brotherhood: "We can get justice and right dealing, only if we put as of paramount importance the principle of treating a man on his worth as a man, rather than with reference to his social position, his occupation or the class to which he belongs. We judge a man by his conduct, that is by his character, and not by his wealth or intellect. It is the man's moral quality, his attitude toward the great questions which concern all humanity, his cleanliness of life, his power to do his duty toward himself and toward others, which really count. The noblest of all forms of government is self-government, but it is the most difficult." And then the President asks for justice, and measures to stop debauching the Indians of today with drink, and to educate the Indian mothers to bring up their children rightly.

No man should tear down that of the now, unless he be ready, with his own hands, to help build for that to come. There is no wrong so great but there is a remedy big enough to overcome it; no decay without a new life at hand, ready to blossom forth. Many Masons complain of the failures of Masonry to make real Masons, but they mostly propose no relief worked out. The blue lodge is, above all, the place for reform. There would I labor. I would fain take all the brethren away from that old dreary path, worn and dust-beaten, stony from the tramp, tramp of candidates, who are ground out along its course year after year without right teaching- for the sake of a "record," or to make the lodge treasury richer. Was it all done for the brotherhood? I would fain take you by the path which leads to the smiling and cheerful fields of true Masonic brotherhood. I will, in short, offer you a remedy. Our lodges are too large, particularly those in the cities. I was a member of the largest one in the state for years and have never known and never expect to know all the brethren of that lodge, nor will they know each other. We are strangers and have not the close and binding ties we read of in the monitors. It is physically impossible for any officers, no matter how good they are, nor how much money they spend, to bring together members scattered over the earth, nor to get those at home to listen to the most sympathetic letters from those away; and perfunctory letters from the secretary, because it is his duty, do no good. Yet, brethren, we continue to insist that a large, rich lodge is strongest and that it will cause true friendship to exist among those who might otherwise have remained at a perpetual distance! Do you not agree, it is absurd to talk that way, when one member does not even know the very existence of another of his own lodge, or merely knows there is a name on the list representing somebody he does not know? It is the lithe, alert, watchful and smaller man, who almost always wins the race against a large, clumsy and unwieldy opponent. Take off your hat to the active small lodge every time. I have always found more real heart there.

On the rolls of Masonry, those lodges will stand highest in which not some few, but each and every member cheerfully gives of his time and labors to make the others happier, not some of the time, but all of the time. I believe in a short while you will see, as I do, that the lodge which succeeds best is the one that limits its membership to say one hundred or less, and whose dues are only enough to pay its running expenses, but which keeps a fund freely contributed by its brethren at each meeting, sacred alone to the relief of the worthy, and unknown to the world in its distribution. Let it join with other lodges in a comfortable and dignified Masonic temple home. Let us see a lodge whose members press forward as one man. What ho, boys. Brother John is down! Then hand to his back and up with him! All together now- steady his feet. Our strength is his and his strength is ours. There, he walks- hurrah, he is safe! Then on with the battle of life, we're shoulder to shoulder again. Softly there, boys, Bro. John can no longer take his place. He has gone down the long path. Come hither and bid him reverently a godspeed. Then do for those he left behind as you would for him. Our strength is still his and the strength of his character is still ours. So on with the battle of life again, we're all together yet, and just as strong.

Build up a lodge where the brethren do not have so much

work that they cannot gather at stated times, and every man knows his brother and, by knowing him, deals kindly with his faults and stands by him in times of sickness, distress and peril; a lodge where the brethren can learn more of the true meaning of Masonry; in short, a lodge based on the family idea, which is the very foundation of this country, and should be the true and firm Masonic foundation. The members of a good family know each other well and stand by each other, as I would have a good Masonic lodge do, and it would do, if mercenary motives be done away with. Now it is perfunctory duty with a large number. No army will ever gain victory if it has company units too large for proper training and management, and the acquaintance of individuals with each other. Armies which fail in these respects have suffered their country to be conquered by the invader. As the civil armies need discipline and education, as individuals and as companies, for greater service, so does the Masonic army need it in as great a degree, lest the broad dominions of Masonry fall before the unworthy invader. I believe our grand lodges could do no greater service than to work out this plan and encourage the formation of lodges of uniform size and not too large. It would make an *esprit de corps*, a Masonic spirit, not to be gained otherwise. Lodges of the kind I picture would not only make Masonry better, but make our cities and our great states and country better, as their influence for good would be felt among all men as among Masons, and so should it be.

XII

EPILOGUE

Listen to the voices of the dim past, and we hear Confucius teaching of a heaven and reverence for ancestors; Zarathrustra, the Persian Christ, telling the people of Ahuramazda, the wise Lord, and Ahriman, the spirit of evil; the Hindu, pointing to a trinity of Brahma the Creator, Vishnu the Preserver and Siva the Destroyer, while the Christian has built up a religion like the composite column, whose beliefs, like the different architectural ideas in the column, embrace all the older ones. Therefore in his song he tells you the same old story:

> Or if on joyful wing.
>> Cleaving the sky;
> Sun, moon and stars forgot.
>> Upward I fly.
> Still all my song shall be.
>> Nearer my God to thee.

O, Redman, art thou of the brotherhood? Is the voice of thy God like any of theirs? Toward what beyond wings thy soul its way?

Me-wi-ja, a long time ago, Paleface. Before many, many great suns; in times of which the paleface tribes know not their own story; all the lands, from one great sea water to the other great sea water, belonged to my people: The buffalo were plentiful as the leaves in summer. Fish filled every stream. Through big, dark forests and over wide plains roamed the deer and all kinds of game. Many swift ponies we had, and there was hunting ground for every tribe. Where the tepees stood, grew our corn. The wanderer who came on peaceful way never stretched forth his hand for corn and venison and was turned aside hungry and footsore. It is truth that the tribes fought with one another over many very little things. So did the palefaces quarrel for things no greater than those about which we quarreled. But we were all Redmen and brethren. This we knew. At last came the palefaces and made, close together, wood and stone houses, upon our rivers and in the midst of our best hunting grounds. They made the big trees to fall, until the plains and hills were bare. On the rivers went their smoke canoes, and over the land very fast went their smoke wagons. With thunder sticks they killed our game. Their medicine men had speaking leaves. Their ways were not ours of the old times, when we roamed here free and happy. First came few palefaces, then more, until their numbers were greater than ever the buffaloes came. Always farther away they drove us. At last, there was little land left where we could hunt. They brought us fire-water, which the Redman never knew. It burned his head and made him crazy, so he did many things he ought not to have done. The palefaces had forked tongues- they lied to my people. We were simple and met them as friends- we offered them the pipe of peace; said we would be their brothers. With deceit they made us help one of their thieving bands to destroy another, because each wanted more trade from us. They broke the faith with us. A prayer they learned of their medicine men who had the bad hearts, and with the prayer they brought down upon us evil spirits. These overcame us, so that we no longer grew strong like the great oaks, but were blown away like straw before a little breeze. In the stillness of the night, oh Paleface, I heard in the moaning wind the voice of thy grandfather as he spoke to my grandfather, saying these words of bitterness:

Listen! Now I have come to step over your soul. You are of the wolf clan. Your spittle I have put at rest under the earth. Your soul I have put at rest under the earth. I have come to cover you over with the black rock. I have come to cover you over with the black cloth. I have come to cover you up with the black slabs, never to reappear. Toward the black coffin of the upland, in the Darkening Land, your paths shall stretch out. So let it be for you. The clay of the upland has come to cover you. Instantly the black clay has lodged there, where it is at rest at the black houses in the Darkening Land. With the black coffin and with the black slabs I have come to cover you. Now your soul has faded away. It has become blue. When darkness comes, your spirit shall grow less and dwindle away, never to reappear.

Our fathers and grandfathers in great numbers now follow the hunt, yonder in the twilight land, where palefaces say is their place of wages and rest.

We now live in peace, but they lode not on us as brothers, though we are few and can no longer harm them. Is this the Masonry of which they boast? Have we not as much brotherhood as they?

Palefaces tell of voices my people know not- say we have many gods. It is not true. We have many names, that is all. You have a Great Spirit- for his name you hang in your lodge an emblem. You also call him by many names. However he may be called, he is but one for the Paleface and the Redman. I tell you how. The Redman knows the forest, where the squirrel gathers nuts for the winter, where the beavers build their houses. The red deer and the buffalo mistake not their trails. The bear surely finds the berries, and the bees their nests. The wild goose tells his way in time to the south summer country. The sky and the earth are brought together by the pathway of the rain and grow warm in each other's embrace, while the sun father looks down to see in wide valleys and plains the seeds spring up and new life arise everywhere, among creatures spread over a great country. The snow-water rivers send down their floods. The animals no longer sleep- the birds fly among the trees. By and by comes the time of ripening com, and mists go up like cold breath. Then the leaves fall, white snow covers the ground- all is once more still until we rise again.

Go, paleface, yonder where leaps the great waters of Yellowstone for many lengths, over the side of the high mountain. The roar of his dashings is heard for much distance. A long time ago, those heights staggered- the mountains reeled, the plains boomed and crackled under the floods and fires- the high hollow places, hugged of men and creatures, were black and awful, so that these grew crazed with fear- tried alike to escape or to hide more deeply. The world rocked with earthquake and thunder. The glass cliff raised its head- there was the roar of swift storms in the northland. The earth was ripped open, ghosts and demons of blackness writhed forth in hot flames from the chasm. The mighty

Teton Range was born. They burst before the eye- the thunder rolled and echoed about them. But ere while all grew deafened and deadened, forgetful, asleep. A tree lighted by the lightning burns not long. Down in the great valley, where lived the dwarf Indians, the water below moved and bubbled, and sent forth high spouts, heated by fires within. Rising, uplifted, are the smoke clouds. So the world was at last alight with sunshine, and bending above was the rainbow. There, ghostly hands painted the edges of the pools- made steps of beadwork like the frozen rainbow, beneath it. There was Nokomis, our mother earth, born with great throes, and so does she rest now, until she shall again burst forth with destruction- her bosom be once more changed before the face of all creatures.

Our Mide sits on the mountain, the better to talk with the Great Spirit. His power raises the Mide to be a Manido, from which point he sees many secrets hidden in the earth. As he watches the dawn come into the sky, high flies the eagle over rock and crag, toward the sun, with earth speeding from under him. The "spirit in the middle" sees him- the Mide is able to reach into the sky- to have from Kitshi Manido the means to lengthen his life. Masonry is with the Redman. In and through and above all these things I tell to you- and with me- is the unseen, all-strong, Atius Tirawa, whose house is in the sky, and whose messenger is the eagle that rides on the wind. Look toward the east; there, there, is Manibozho, the Spirit of Light of the Dawn, the Great White One! Paleface, I have spoken!

THE END